It's time for a change. Where to go? Why Cranberry Portage, a small town in northern Canada…

Randy Roman is on a road trip over the Canadian prairies to her childhood home in a too-small car with two grumpy nephews, an enthusiastic puppy and her mother's ashes in the trunk. She just can't pinpoint that moment her life started running wild.

Her teenage nephew **Eric** keeps his head buried in a sketchbook, hoping that at any moment his aunt will come to her senses and turn the car around. In the meantime, he's comfortable drowning out his baby brother with rock and roll.

Roadside detours are young **Mickey**'s specialty. His fascination with dragonflies, dinosaurs and all this trip has to offer reminds Randy of the iridescent quality of childhood.

After cashing in his pension, **Tom Webb** fills his days canoeing the pristine waters of Cranberry Portage where he purchases a beautiful old house ripe for renovations. He doesn't want to be a richer man, just a different man. How was he supposed to know that he'd acquired Randy's family's ancestral home, and that kismet was about to occur once aunt, nephews, dog and mother arrived in town?

Kate Austin

Kate Austin has worked as a legal assistant, a commercial fisher, a brewery manager, a teacher, a technical writer and a herring popper, while managing to read an average of a book a day. Go ahead—ask her anything. If she doesn't know the answer, she'll make it up because she's been reading and writing fiction for as long as she can remember.

She blames her mother and her two grandmothers for her reading and writing obsession—all of them were avid readers and they passed the books and the obsession on to her. She lives in Vancouver, Canada, where she can walk on the beach whenever necessary, even in the rain.

She'd be delighted to hear from readers through her Web site: www.kateaustin.ca.

dragonflies AND dinosaurs
KATE AUSTIN

DRAGONFLIES AND DINOSAURS

copyright © 2005 Kate Austin

i s b n 0 3 7 3 8 8 0 7 4 X

TheNextNovel.com

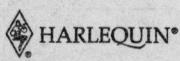 HARLEQUIN®

PRINTED IN U.S.A.

This book is for my mother.
I wish she was here to read it.

Acknowledgment

People too numerous to thank helped me get
this far, but there are a few I have to mention:
Russell Brown, who taught me what writing really was;
Terry, who told me for years I could do it and eventually
managed to convince me; Heather and Patrick, who
always made me laugh even when they were critical about
my work; everyone at NST, who allowed me to write
when things were slow, paid me for it and encouraged
me every step of the way; Ardella, my first reader. And
finally, Mary Louise Schwartz, my agent, because she
loved this book so much and she took a chance on me.
Thanks to all of you, because I wouldn't
be here without you.

CHAPTER 1

Dragonflies live two different lives, in two different worlds. The young dragonfly begins its life in the water, eventually crawling out of the pond to transform itself into a superb aerial hunter with a wing span as big as 7.5 inches across.
—*The Sunshine Coast News*, September 14, 2005

We measured our progress by red-tailed hawks and the iridescent carcasses of dragonflies flickering against the windshield in the warm light of the setting sun.

Eric and I counted the hawks, learning, as we crossed the endless prairie miles, to recognize their call, the broad silhouette of their wings in flight, and to spot them sitting still as death on fence posts and telephone poles. At each stop—for gas, for food, for a cheap, sometimes clean motel—Mickey analyzed, bagged and recorded the wings stuck in the florid yellow smudges on the windshield. And then he carefully cleaned the glass until it reflected, without a flaw, the flaming prairie sun.

The wings were all that remained of the dragonflies after their abrupt halt against our windshield. Mickey used my eyebrow tweezers to tug them from the baked-on sludge surrounding them. He was extraordinarily patient, his wiry body stretched out over the boiling hood of the car, the tweezers in one hand, a plastic container in the other. I watched him. No longer a little boy, his face had thinned out over the past weeks, grown definition and character. His white T-shirt and shorts, even his untanned skin, vanished into the milky haze of prairie heat. His short dark hair and matching eyes remained, burning holes in the air between us.

Mickey's obsession with this form of violent death made me nervous. So did Eric's silence. And the huge blue cloudless bowl of the sky above us, day after perfect day, made me want to crawl into a cave.

The white lines disappearing beneath the car gave me the heebie-jeebies—one, two, three, four. Break. One, two, three, four. Another break. Mickey counted out loud, and my head rang to the sound of his voice. One, two. Three, four. Pause. I'd get used to one rhythm, then he'd change it. One. Two, three, four. Pause. One, two, three. Four. But I couldn't ask him to stop.

When he did stop, that made me nervous too. I turned my head to check that he was okay. He had pulled earphones over his ears, closed his eyes and vanished into the music. I rolled up my window to shut out the sound of the highway and heard the faint tinny sounds of Limp Bizkit.

I glanced in the rearview mirror. Eric shrugged and turned back to his sketchbook, drawing God knows what. The one glimpse I'd had of his sketch pad since we left home, before he shut it in my face, was a drawing of a tiger devouring a fawn, in excruciating detail and vibrant, unreal colors. I couldn't remember the last time he'd spoken.

We weren't moving fast. Not with two boys aged twelve and fifteen. They slept until noon, insisted on showers and full breakfasts. By then it was past lunchtime. Finally on the road, we didn't make time; we made pit stops. The car filled up with sticky slurpy cups and rattling aluminum cans.

On this trip two hundred kilometers was a good day's journey, even across the straight-lined prairies. I bit my tongue and pulled into another rest stop, gas station or tourist attraction. I handed over money for drinks, food, admission. I stopped at a bank machine at least once a day.

The idea for this journey had begun in a brightly lit hospital room two weeks ago on the day we learned that my sister, their mother, wasn't going to die.

I choked on the sour taste of vomit filling my mouth. The smell did it, antiseptic laden with a hint of stale bodies and still-warm spilled blood. That smell and the memories it brought with it. The walls were covered with battleship-gray latex, but no scraping, no cleaning, no paint could disguise the strip of pain running along the corridor, hand-high, where patients and their visitors touched the walls, leaving tiny molecules of anguish behind.

I felt it rising from beneath the layers. I kept my hands clenched in my pockets because I couldn't bear to touch the walls.

The good news was that this time the patient wouldn't die. Or so the doctors said, assuring us that the system was working, that detection saved Susan's life. Not early enough to save her breasts, but early enough for life. I had trouble believing, my faith in the medical system severely shaken when my young and seemingly healthy mother had gone into the hospital two years ago and never come out.

My mother's nurses and doctors had told me her moans meant nothing. The medication took care of the pain. But the moans meant something to me. They meant I couldn't sleep for the fourteen days it took her to die, nor for almost a month after. Even now, I often woke to ghostly moans from the spare bedroom. Opening its door, I expected to see my mother lying on the bed, surrounded by flickering red monitor lights and moaning in the chill antiseptic air. Now Susan lay in the surgical ward of the same hospital.

She smiled and beckoned me in when I knocked tentatively at her door. We looked enough alike to be twins, although I was older by a year and Susan's once-glowing, healthy skin now appeared gray and muddy. But, despite these differences, no one could mistake our shared genes.

This, basically, was what I worried about. Every minute of every day since my mother went into the hospital. There had been no need for my mother to die of breast cancer, not if she'd followed recommendations and had a mammogram every year, or seen a doctor when she started feeling sick. But not my mother—no doctors or hospitals for her. She died because of who she was.

That's what the doctors said. That's what Susan and I said. But Susan believed it and I didn't. So it didn't help me much. Just set me wondering how many women died of curable diseases because, like my mother, they'd had their children in the days when natural childbirth meant hours, sometimes days, of pain.

Susan had the operation and was going home in a few days to start healing and then chemo, probably radiation after that. She, unlike our mother, caught the lumps before they spread throughout her body. I was specially tested twice, ultrasounds and everything, in addition to my monthly self-examination and my yearly mammogram. Everything negative—but the pages of positive results, the unequivocal good health I enjoyed, didn't convince me. No reassurance cracked the thick layer of anxiety I carried.

I imagined lying in the hospital bed. I visualized every step of the operation removing my breasts. It got so I even felt the shunt in my lymph glands, and the bruising in my armpits. I imagined the day the surgeon came to tell me all hope was gone. I pictured his face, sad and forlorn because he loved me, and there was nothing he could do.

I imagined my deathbed, the flowers and cards, the crying friends and family. I went to my own funeral. And I didn't do this once; I did it almost every night. I woke up in the darkest hours of the night and started right in at the beginning, with the hospital bed. I couldn't sleep until I'd imagined the funeral. My elaborate fantasy felt more real than reality.

Forty-two years old and I was obsessed with my own imminent death, even though every indicator said I was fine, perfectly healthy. But I didn't believe. I couldn't.

None of this showed in my face, or at least I hoped it didn't. Susan's life held enough complications without worrying about her sister. Besides, I was the strong one, the older, more mature, in-control one. Stiff upper lip, that was me. No one knew that underneath my cheerful exterior lay a quivering mass of fear and anxiety. Especially not my baby sister. Especially not now.

Because today was D-day. Time to hear the results of the desperate operation to save Susan's life. I timed my visit to arrive after rounds and the pronouncement of the verdict. Life? Or death? One look at her face and I knew.

She was going to be fine. Fine, that is, if you didn't count the months to come. Near-death while they killed her cancer with radiation and drugs so virulent that her body would almost die with it. And there were no guarantees. We'd wait and watch for five years and still might not know. I tried to ignore the statistics on life expectancy and recurrence and to believe, with Susan, that she would be okay. Even though I couldn't do the same for myself.

I stood at the door, tears running down my face, dripping onto my yellow silk blouse until I looked as if I'd dropped not just a glass but an entire bottle of white wine onto my breasts. The blouse would never be the same but I would hang it, untouched and uncleaned, in the back of my closet, leave it there as mute evidence of a miracle.

Susan's courage, and mine, flagged as the doctors enumerated the cost of living. What about the boys? My nephews? The loves of my life? How could she ask them to watch her through weeks filled with needles and diarrhea, moaning and vomiting? How could Susan concentrate on recovery with Mickey and Eric on summer vacation? She had spent the morning coming up with a solution.

"It's the reunion this summer," Susan said.

I nodded. I'd had what felt like hundreds of reminders of it. At least once a week I opened my mailbox to another mimeographed newsletter headed "Cranberry Portage Reunion." It was filled with news about people I didn't know and didn't care to, cute poems in iambic pentameter, badly reproduced photographs of places I'd long forgotten.

My mother would have gone to the reunion and, for her sake, I flipped through the newsletters before I threw them away. The years in Cranberry Portage were the best years of her life. She'd spent years telling me so, bemoaning her loss, reminding me of events and people I didn't want to remember. Everything in our lives suffered by comparison. She filled Susan and I with fairy tales about a town and a man so perfect they couldn't possibly exist—not in the harsh realm of northern Manitoba. Maybe not anywhere.

"Take the boys," Susan continued, "and drive across. The prairies are beautiful in the summer and you haven't had a vacation since Mum died. You haven't taken your car out of the city once since you bought it and it's a perfect ride for a long trip, smooth, cheap on gas." Susan was a mechanic, one of the few female ones in the city, and made way more money than me. "You know I'm right. You need a break. You can do some sight-seeing, go to the dinosaur museum, hike in the mountains, maybe even do a little canoeing."

My face must have reflected my distress.

"My car doesn't need four thousand miles of highway time. And neither do I. Besides, the three of us would spend all our time arguing about music. Eric only listens to those whatever-you-call-em bands, Limp Bizkit and Korn. I hate them. Nope. Bad idea." I rubbed my temples. I got a headache just thinking about it.

The last place I wanted to visit was Cranberry Portage. I was six when we moved to the Coast. My memories of that town were buried so deep I couldn't dig them out in a month of Sundays. I cringed when I heard myself use my mother's expression. I'd made a life without a father, without a man, a life I was perfectly happy about, and that was that. I didn't need to go back to some supposedly idyllic childhood I couldn't remember.

"They'll hate it," I said, "and Mickey always gets carsick."

"Not if he's in the front seat. I'll give you a year's supply of motion-sickness patches to take with you. Please, Randy. I don't want them to see me when I'm sick. The operation was one thing, but that was short-term and they can see I'm okay. I can fake it for visiting hours. But I won't be able to do that with the chemotherapy. They'll be so scared I'll use all my energy making them feel better. Just take them and have a good time."

"But..."

The next couple of hours remained indistinct in my memory, as if Susan's surgeon had excised them from my life, leaving a vacant space to match her now-vanished breasts. I remembered the existence of those hours but had no ability to imagine them into being.

All I knew was that sometime during those two hours I consented to take the boys to Cranberry Portage and I spilled the beans about my job. Instead of me comforting her, I ended up with my head on the bed, next to her breastless bosom, her hands in my hair, whining over my lost job and my suddenly rudderless life. Me. Miranda Jane Roman. Pouring out my sorrows to my baby sister. Unheard-of. Pathetic.

Both the sorrows and the pouring out of them were new to me. I'd spent my life smiling, putting on a happy face, until now, in early middle age, my face settled automatically into cheeriness.

I'd spent my free time—and I had way too much of it since I got laid off—in front of a mirror, practicing a more appropriate expression. I aimed for a sombre middle-aged oh-I've-lost-my-job-after-twenty-years kind of look. It didn't work. I tried surprise. Despair. Panic. Even though I felt those things, my face refused to reflect my unhappiness. The mirror reproduced my round face, bright eyes (no matter that they were bright with tears), and snub nose, my upturned lips and laugh lines. I looked like a woman without a care in the world.

I tried choosing the harshest light. Cold fluorescent tubes. And the green walls of the women's washroom on the surgical ward at Saint Paul's Hospital. I stood in front of the mirror, my face sallow in the harsh, clear light, and replayed the worst day of my life.

Nine in the morning. I'm at my desk, trying to separate fact from fiction in Ross McKay's highly creative loan application. The phone rings, startling me out of my rapt perusal of an improbable profit-and-loss statement.

"Randy Roman," I say, in my professional voice. There is a pause at the other end of the phone line, then a voice, which sounds familiar but which I can't place for a period of time that feels like forever but is really only fifteen words long.

"Hi. I got the results of my mammogram today. I'm scheduled for surgery right away." *My sister Susan.*

Now the pause is at my end while I search, desperately, for a response.

"Um." It's all I can think of, all I can bear to say. Every other word in the English language will mean too much. Or too little.

"The boys are at school. Can you pick them up? I'm admitted already. Saint Paul's, of course. Room ten-eleven. Randy? Okay?"

I nod but it doesn't get through to her. She keeps talking.

"Randy? Are you there?"

I'm nodding my head like an idiot. The phone is clasped so tightly that my knuckles are white against its blackness and my arm quivers with the strain. I evade the fear and venture a response.

"Yes."

"Can you pick them up? Stay at our place for a while? Maybe two weeks, but we won't know for sure until after the operation. And then there's the chemotherapy. And, well, you know. Whatever else." Her voice dies away, swallowed up in the pain to come.

"Yes," I say again.

Susan's voice returns, strong and sure, as she tells me what time to pick up the boys after school. I respond to her confidence.

"I'll pick them up. I'll stay for as long as you need me."

I take a deep breath and promise to do the one thing that scares me almost as much as Susan's news. The hospital. I have spent two years avoiding it, crossing the street to pass by on the other side, driving blocks out of my way, sending flowers and balloons to my friends having babies or minor operations instead of visiting.

"I'll be at the hospital in a couple of hours, just have to clear up my desk. Susan, are you okay?" Stupid question, but she sounds so strong. I want her to reassure me.

I want her to tell me that the will in her safe-deposit box can stay there, that I won't become the sole guardian of my nephews. That I won't lose her the way I did my mother. But of course I can't ask her any of these things. She responds to my unvoiced panic.

"I'm fine. They think I'll be okay."

I throw McKay's loan application into my out tray marked with a big red no. There's nothing else urgent on my desk, nothing that the kid in the next office can't handle. I walk down the hall to Human Resources and go through the usual gauntlet of assistants and form-filling before I'm allowed the privilege of sitting down across the desk from Mr. Vice President Human Resources. He has a name—Tony Hall—but it's impossible to think of him without his title.

"Tony, I need a leave of absence. My sister has cancer, and I have to take care of her kids.

He just looks at me.

"I've been with the bank for twenty years," I continue. "I checked my vacation entitlement and I'm owed four weeks. But I might need longer than that."

"That shouldn't be a problem." He hands me an ominous-looking envelope I've seen more than once in the hands of others. "You'll have all the time you want."

I've made this easy for Mr. VPHR, no lawsuits, no human-rights tribunals. I've given him an opportunity to look like a nice guy for giving me the time I need.

Twenty years of faithful service turns out to be worth eighteen months' salary and limited benefits.

At the hospital I pretend everything is fine with me, tell Susan the bank happily acquiesced to an indefinite leave of absence. The permanently cheery face comes in handy as I sit beside Susan's bed, her warm hand in mine, and listen to her instructions about the boys' routine.

I nod and write things down in the notebook she hands me as if I haven't been a surrogate parent for the past five years since she and Don split up and he moved to Newfoundland to fish so he couldn't be forced to pay child support. As if I haven't made them dinner, washed their clothes, played baseball and soccer and lacrosse with them. As if I haven't taken them to school, helped them with their homework, fought with their homeroom teachers over slights so trivial they are now forgotten and buried so deep it would take a backhoe to retrieve them. I pretend it's all new to me so Susan can pretend she's still in control of her life.

Waves of nausea roll over me with each breath. I smile. And smile some more, until my face aches with the strain.

Susan asks me for one last favor.

"Bring the boys down during visiting hours. I want them to see I'm okay."

I cringe at the prospect, but how can I refuse?

I race from the hospital to pick up the boys at their respective schools. They don't question my arrival.

There's nothing unusual about finding my white Mazda in the school parking lot. Nor would they question my presence in the kitchen making sloppy joes, my dirty laundry in their washing machine. Situation normal.

"Get in the car," I say, "we're going for a drive."

The hospital is less frightening for me this time because I'm focused on Eric and Mickey walking on each side of me. I've told them where we're going and they're scared. Mickey, who hasn't held my hand since a classmate laughed at him for doing so on the first day of kindergarten, now clasps it so tightly our sweaty palms meld together. And Eric lumbers on the other side, his hands in his pockets, his shoulders hunched over so far he looks like Quasimodo.

Mickey chatters, commenting on everything in a shrill, tight voice. Eric hasn't said a single word since I told them where we were going. I open the door to Susan's room and push them inside. I stand outside with my back to the door, arms crossed under my suddenly aching breasts, and guard Susan's privacy. I prepare to repel any and all intruders while she tells her sons she has cancer.

I don't know what Susan says to them, but the atmosphere is miraculously lightened when Eric pulls open the door and I fall backward into the room, the flowers I carry landing on my chest with a thump and a dusting of pollen that keeps me awake and sneezing all night.

* * *

It didn't take long to replay the worst day of my life but even after the recital, my regular face continued to reflect back at me, cheerful and unconcerned. There was, obviously, no way to change it, no way to make it mirror the inside reality of my life. And standing there in the hospital washroom, I wondered about the rest of the world. About all those other happy faces I saw in restaurants and movie theaters. Were they like me? And what about those long-faced people I avoided? What if, under their dour exteriors, lay contentment? Maybe even joy? My mother always said *you have to take people at face value*. I began to think she might have been wrong about that, beginning to believe instead, *you can't judge a book by its cover*.

I smiled at myself in the sickly green light and went back to Susan's room for the celebration, the bottle of champagne heavy in my shoulder bag. When I pushed open the door, Susan's surgeon, a tall blond man who looked as if he skied for a living rather than spent it standing in bright artificial light up to his elbows in blood and guts, stood beside her bed, holding her hand. He looked at her as if she still had breasts, and she looked back at him as if it didn't matter that she didn't. I backed out of the room and once again took up guard duty.

No man ever looked at me that way. Not even my no-account boyfriend when he tried to convince me that the damage to my brand-new car wasn't his fault even if the police report and the insurance company insisted it was. Even my mother had never looked at me with unconditional love. Or had she?

That thought haunted me. What if she had always loved me and I had refused to see it? What if our estrangement was based on an incorrect premise? I felt guilty enough about it without learning I was the one who had caused it. Over the past five years, I had been on speaking terms with my mother for exactly two weeks, the two weeks it took her to die. The words that had started the fight between us were lost in the mists of time. Even I no longer remembered them. I tried, because I wanted to confirm my position, to assuage my guilt, but they were lost and would stay that way.

I might have broken the silence a million times. We were often in the same house—family birthdays, Christmas, Thanksgiving—but I became adept at avoiding her, moving from room to room just ahead of her. After the first couple of years, she played the game with me, and it got easier.

Now, though, I pictured those events and my behavior with shame. I gave myself credit for staying by her side while she died, but I knew that wouldn't redeem me. Not even close.

The sun sat even with the rear window, Eric's head casting a huge dark shadow forward into the front seat, dividing me from Mickey.

Day six, 650 kilometers into the journey, and I was hot, tired and cranky. And so were the boys. At this rate, we'd kill each other before the first week was out. I abandoned my search for a cheap motel and pulled into a brand-new hotel, its sign promising satellite TV, saunas, a wave pool and a video arcade. A faint smile passed, fleetingly, over Mickey's face, and the chill emanating from the back seat receded.

Eric's Notebook

Mum is sick, really sick. She says she's okay, but I think she's dying. That's why she sent us away. So I'm stuck in the car with Mickey and Randy. I should be at home. Mum needs me.

Every time I open my mouth I think I'm going to puke. My stomach feels like a washing machine. I'm not carsick, not like Mickey. I'd like it in the car if everything wasn't such a mess. I can't close my eyes. All I can think about is Mum, and the way she looked in the hospital.

She had tubes in her hands and nose, and her hands were bruised. The whites of her eyes were yellow. And she didn't move, not even a bit. She looked like a dead person.

I know what Mickey's doing. He's talking, talking, talking. Because he thinks if he fills all

the empty spaces, no one will know he's scared.
But I know.

I can't draw. I put the lines on the page.
They kind of look like something. But they don't
look like what they're supposed to. They're all
muddy and loose. Unconnected. I'm losing Mum.
And now I can't draw.

Randy's a mess. She can barely drive. I wish
I was sixteen. Then I could drive. Maybe I'd feel
safe then. Everything is a mess. My whole life is
falling apart.

CHAPTER 2

When collecting dragonflies, keep each live specimen in a separate container, otherwise you might
end up with only tattered wings when you arrive
home. Tupperware is a good working tool for collecting as it keeps the specimens dry and does not
crush in your backpack.
—*The Sunshine Coast News*, September 14, 2005

Day One

Eight o'clock. I'd been up all night packing and re-
packing the car. Trying to get everything that might
possibly be needed by a woman accustomed to reading
five or six books a week, and two teenage boys who lived
in a house full of computers, TVs, stereo equipment,
games, bikes, comics, a trampoline, pool table, two
overfull refrigerators, and a freezer as big as my second
bedroom, for a trip whose duration was as yet un-
determined, crammed into a two-door Mazda, and still

leave enough room for the three of us to drive across the country in comfort. Or at least not in total discomfort.

I opened the trunk, took everything out, again, right down to the spare tire, and piled it on the pavement. I laid down the law the night before, when the boys finally went to bed long after midnight. One small suitcase each (we'd do laundry as we went along), and a second bag containing personal items. I should have specified the size.

Eric handed me his hockey kit bag without a word, Mickey an old camouflage duffel, which belonged first to my father, then Mickey's mother. Mine, bought on a trip to Mexico five years ago, rivaled both of theirs in size. No way I'd get all three suitcases and the bags in the trunk. Forget the cooler I placed hopefully on the pile. I settled for four out of six and slung Eric's bag into the back seat, along with Mickey's. I abandoned the pillows; they could use the bags to cushion their heads.

One last thing and I, at least, was ready. The sun beat down on my tired and aching head. In my arms, I cradled the small, square, gray plastic tub containing my mother.

Susan reminded me of her. The ashes had been placed on the bookshelf in my living room months ago. For the year after I picked her up at the crematorium she traveled with me in the trunk of my car, only making it into the house when I sold the car and emptied the trunk. I liked having her there with me in that form, maybe because the one story I remembered her telling that wasn't fraught with nostalgia for the past was about her father's ashes. She carried him in the trunk of her car for months until she got stopped at the border for a routine check during a terrorist scare.

"Open your trunk, please."

She opened it. The trunk had, over the years, acquired the flavor of my mother's spare bedroom, full of castoffs and garage-sale possibilities that would never see the light of day, let alone get sold. It took fifteen minutes to empty the trunk onto the hot pavement.

A broken lawn chair she had bought for fifty cents and planned to repair. Two bags of potting soil, one with a minute hole in the corner, dusting everything around it with mica and rich brown dirt. A box of mismatched china. Green garbage bag full of winter coats infested with mothballs. Five purses containing various forgotten lipsticks, compacts and dried-up tubes of mascara.

By this time, she said, the car was surrounded by customs guards. There were ten or twelve of them, towering over her, their hands hovering at their gun belts, the sun reflecting off their sunglasses. They waited while the youngest and least experienced of them continued to pull things from the trunk.

Three boxes of old canning jars, sans lids and sealers, full of desiccated bugs and wisps of cobwebs. My father's old uniform rolled up in a ball, which, when unrolled, released a horde of moths into the still air of August.

Finally the trunk was empty, but the troop of guards didn't move, turning their empty eyes from my mother to the sweating guard who had pulled these things from the trunk, as if he were responsible for the objects he'd touched. Nothing was said but the young guard looked at the car in something like despair until, Mum said, a light went on in his head. She actually saw the moment he realized what they wanted him to do.

He quickly, even eagerly, pulled the filthy carpet from the floor of the trunk, flung the spare tire to the pavement, and picked up an unlabeled cardboard box, carefully sealed with packing tape. He shook it. By this time a dog had arrived and was straining at his leash, sniffing at the soil, sneezing at the mothballs, and ignoring the cardboard box. This didn't stop the guards who, with an almost imperceptible nod at the young one, handed him an exacto knife with a bright yellow plastic handle. It looked like a child's toy in his hand. He slit the tape, pulled open the top of the box, bent down and offered it to the dog, who turned away without interest and returned to peeing on the tire.

The young guard handed the box to the guard with the darkest glasses, most severe expression and the biggest belly, not to mention the biggest gun. Not a single word had been spoken since the first "Open your trunk, please."

So my mother was delighted to hear him speak, pleased to know he could.

"What is it?" he asked, holding a handful of gray dust to his nose and sniffing lightly. She watched him touch his tongue to the dust.

"Oh, there he is," my mother said. "It's my father's ashes. I've been looking for them forever."

I loved this story, always waiting impatiently for the punch line, imagining the expression on the guard's face as he realized what was in his mouth. My mother, a storyteller from way back, stopped right there, allowing me to imagine what happened next. I spent hours trying on alternate endings, never needing or wanting to know the official version. I knew, even then, that my imagination was better than reality.

"Take her home with you," Susan had said, "to Paint Lake. She loved it there. You and the boys can canoe in and scatter her ashes. There's nowhere she'd rather be."

I knew Susan was right, but I wasn't sure if I could put her back in the car. I'd grown accustomed to her presence in my living room. I, who had never owned even a fish, let alone a bird or a cat or a dog, talked to her. I was determined to make up for five years' worth of silence. I told her everything. About my day at work, the movies I saw, books I read, the very few men I met. She never answered me, but once in a while I felt as if she were about to.

I stood by the car, trying to decide whether to take her on the trip, and thinking about the rest of my conversation with Susan.

"Paint Lake?" I questioned. "Where in the hell is that?"

It pissed me off that Susan might know something about our mother I didn't, even though, given the extra years she had to talk to her, it shouldn't have surprised me.

"It's the Cranberry River system, you know, the one the town's named after."

I didn't know. All I knew about Cranberry Portage and vicinity was what I'd learned from the reunion newsletters and from my mother's nostalgic and highly colored stories, which I tuned out so perfectly I remembered few, if any, details.

"I haven't canoed for two summers."

"Doesn't matter. Eric's the assistant scout instructor now, and Mickey's not far behind. You'll be fine with them."

My protests, like those over the trip itself, were useless. I grudgingly consented to take my mother with us, silently reserving the right to bring her back. I wasn't so sure she didn't belong right there on my bookshelf. I tucked the tub into the corner of the trunk, closed it and stepped back to admire my handiwork. Everything neatly stowed and plenty of room left for a boy five sizes larger than most fifteen-year-olds and a twelve-year-old for whom the opposite was true. I clapped my hands in satisfaction and marched into the house, passing through the kitchen with a startled glance at the clock. Almost eleven.

The room at the top of the stairs exuded an air of sullen silence as if to say *don't even think about waking us*.

I opened the door. They'd spent one night in my spare bedroom and it bore the unmistakable funk of boy—sweat and old socks and spilled Pepsi, mingled with odors I chose not to identify. It was dark and warm and moist like the inside of a sauna. I stood next to the bed and watched them sleep.

I used to do this when they were babies. I'd watch them breathing, their little noses, with those perfect baby lips, the top one curved like a bow, and the fontanels throbbing under delicate hair, smelling like baby powder and clean sheets. They would breathe short and panting, then they would sigh, great dream-filled sighs, and start all over again. And when they were just about to wake up, they would open their eyes and look around, surprised, as if they'd come from another world and crash-landed in their cribs.

When they noticed me, they always smiled. I loved that moment, because they would be so excited at the idea of getting out of bed and starting a new day. They thrashed around with their arms and legs, reaching out to me until I picked them up.

Those babies were still visible in the sleeping faces in my spare bedroom, and I couldn't bear to wake them because I understood why they insisted on staying asleep. I would have done it myself if I could sleep at all. Sleeping meant they didn't have to remember why we were in this situation. Sleeping meant they could forget their mother's bruised face and body. They could forget their fear.

I pulled the door closed behind me and went downstairs for a cup of tea and one of the raspberry muffins I'd bought last night. So we wouldn't have to stop for snacks. Huh.

Then another muffin. And a cup of tea. And another muffin and another until the bag was empty and the sun had moved through the sky and was on the first leg of its downward slide into night before I heard movement from up the stairs. Not just movement, but screaming.

"Me first."

"No, me. You went first yesterday."

"No, you did."

"You did."

I could have told them who went first yesterday, and the day before, and the day before that, but I stayed in the kitchen.

The crash of a chair—I hoped it was a chair and not a body—accompanied the heavy thump-thump of Eric's feet into the bathroom. Eric, by right of being firstborn, a foot taller, and fifty pounds heavier, almost always got to the bathroom first. He got to everything first. And he took full advantage of it.

Mickey did far more than his share of house and

yard work, running to the store for chocolate bars, ice cream or slurpies, washing the car and folding the laundry. Eric never had to tell Mickey to do these things, it happened almost naturally, through a subtle combination of hero worship, bribes and unspoken threats. The threats didn't promise violence, rather a withholding of favor. Mickey was the only little brother entitled to tag along to the BMX track or the DQ. A hint that he'd be left behind was all it took to send him scurrying for the broom or the hose.

Up until the past couple of weeks, the system had worked without tension or resentment on either side. The screaming from the upstairs hallway wasn't my first indication the precarious balance had shifted. The noise combined with my sugar-and-caffeine high, and the late time pushed me over the edge into hysterical laughter.

I couldn't stop. A look at my watch—five o'clock—had me falling off my chair as Mickey, his hair in spikes around his pale, elfin face, came in and sat down across from me. I passed him the box of doughnuts—at some point after I'd finished the muffins I ran down the block for doughnuts for the trip (wishful thinking, it was)—and poured him a glass of orange juice.

He opened the Tim Hortons box and examined the contents. Mickey wasn't a picky eater, but he knew what he liked, and had inherited his stubbornness from his mother. No liver, no onions, and definitely no orange food. No Kraft Dinner—a staple of my childhood—no cheeses, carrots, or orange Jell-O. He looked at the table, discovered the lack of utensils and plates with a start of surprise, waited a few moments to see whether I'd catch on to his dilemma (I did, but ignored it), and, with a sigh, stood up and padded over to the drying rack for a plate, knife and fork.

Mickey, the only person I knew who ate doughnuts with cutlery, placed a chocolate doughnut covered with multicolored sprinkles in the exact center of his plate. He ate as neatly as a cat, each tiny bite precisely sliced away from the doughnut, moving in a ninety-degree arc, then placed on his tongue without touching his lips. Except for the spiky hair, baggy T-shirt and bare feet, he might have been an upper-class English butler showing a junior footman how to eat in front of his betters.

Forty-five minutes later, a quick bathroom interval for Eric, he raced down the stairs and threw himself into a chair. His face was shining and clean, his hair perfectly and exactly styled, a half-inch of dark brown covered with a further half inch of bleached blond. The makers of hair bleach, their market share in decline since the fifties, must have been delighted with the resurgence of the bleaching fad.

Eric grabbed for a jelly doughnut, bit it in half, the pink jelly narrowly missing his fluorescent-yellow

T-shirt, although I doubted anyone would notice if it hadn't, and reached for another while still chomping at the first. The box of a dozen doughnuts disappeared, one-third without leaving a crumb behind to mark their passage, the others a trail Hansel and Gretel could follow in the dark.

We were finally out the door and into the car. I'd checked the stove, taken the garbage out, double-locked the front and back doors, Mickey following behind to make sure I'd done everything necessary, while Eric waited, lounging against the car, his earphones plugged in and his feet moving to whatever hard rock he was playing—although he wavered between classic and contemporary, it was always hard.

We pulled out of the driveway at 7:15 p.m., the sun almost at the horizon. I yawned, once, and then couldn't stop. I'd been up for almost two days and knew I shouldn't be driving. A ninety-minute nap waiting for the boys had given me a too-short second wind, but I wanted to get on the road before the voices clamoring in my head convinced me to abandon the whole project. I drove east into the darkening sky, yawning and hoping that once we got out of the city, out of familiar territory, I wouldn't turn back, but knowing too I only had a couple of hours before it wouldn't be safe to be driving.

The freeway unrolled in the headlights, each exit

sign farther away from my old life. Soon we were traveling through farmland, pasture, raspberry fields. The mountains moved closer, following the highway, cutting off the fading light left in the sky. Mickey sat beside me, his hands folded in his lap, his face serene in the passing headlights. He read the exit and mileage signs out loud, his singsong voice happy even when I didn't answer him. I felt safe with him there, his soft breathing a comforting presence in the dark.

Eric sat in the back, silent, a hulking presence in my rearview mirror. I could hear tinny sounds coming from his earphones but couldn't distinguish the band. I didn't want to.

Mickey read the latest sign, "Hope, next left."

"We'll stay there tonight," I said. "We'll stay in Hope."

CHAPTER 3

Environment plays a large role in insect behavior. Studying dragonflies only in a controlled environment—such as rearing containers—will skew your results. You must take into account their behavior in the wild.
—*The Sunshine Coast News*, September 14, 2005

Day Three

The sun was high in the sky and I was already regretting the lack of air-conditioning as we pulled out of the McDonald's parking lot and onto the highway. My hamburger and fries settled into my stomach like a softball. Eric's earphones didn't quite disguise the music, and I'd heard it often enough to almost but not quite remember the lyrics. It annoyed me. I worried for a minute about hearing loss and then shrugged it off. At least it stopped him from fighting with Mickey.

They never used to fight, something I found amazing, given the way Susan and I grew up. We said our first civil words to each other the day she graduated from British Columbia Institute of Technology. We hadn't been in the same province for almost five years while I went east to university and she finished high school and her apprenticeship program. I phoned home once a week while I was gone—ten o'clock on Sunday morning—knowing she'd still be sleeping.

Her graduation took place on a beautiful sunny day and I had been summoned home for the event. No excuse would be accepted, no way to get out of it. The air smelled like heaven. When I left five years ago, I promised myself I wouldn't come back, telling my new friends, "I'm tired of the mountains," talking about them in my newly discovered literary voice. "They're symbols, wielding the ax of years spent in their shadows." Even I knew how pretentious that sounded but I couldn't help myself. I loved the sound of my own voice.

But as soon as I stepped off the plane I felt safe for the first time in years, surrounded by mountains and clouds and the deep, dark green of the rain forest, settling into the moist, salty air like a cat on a sun-filled windowsill.

Maybe the relief made me walk up to Susan and put my arms around her. Maybe the change in air pressure or the scents of cedar and salt. Whatever caused my abnormal behavior, from that day forward Susan and I became as close friends as we had earlier been staunch enemies.

I hoped the opposite wouldn't be true for Eric and Mickey. Susan said they fought because they were scared and I mostly believed her, but she didn't have to live with it. The squabbling started the day I first took them to the hospital and escalated every day.

This morning brought a new wrinkle. No longer content with flinging words, Eric threw a wet towel. I grabbed it and stepped in between them.

"Stop."

Mickey wore his rebellious face, Eric his sullen one. I replied with my stubborn one. They knew me well enough to gauge the results of any confrontation under these conditions and quickly abandoned all thoughts of continuing.

"Mickey, get in the shower. Now. Eric, pack the car. I'll check us out and meet you in the parking lot."

They were still sparring about breakfast as they came up to the car, although Eric shut up when he got in the back seat. He didn't say much around me anymore. Yes and no comprised practically his entire vocabulary. I turned left and waited for Mickey's official decision on a restaurant. It wasn't a surprise.

He loved McDonald's. I hated it, and I had no idea of how Eric felt, but it was close and fast and I felt a sense of urgency. I wanted to get over the mountains, away from the smell of the hospital. I wanted something new to look at. I wanted to be distracted, engaged, engulfed in something unique, unmistakable, unforgettable. The guidebook promised tunnels and slides, rivers, parks, wildflowers, wildlife. So McDonald's it was. If Eric wouldn't speak, he'd have no vote.

We headed out of the parking lot after breakfast and into a movie world. A couple of nights ago, I rented *First Blood* to show the boys where we were going, remembering only the scenery and forgetting the violence. I didn't need to worry, because the boys loved it, watching it over and over again. They sat in the living room, blinds drawn against the sun, and watched the movie until they knew most of the lines by heart.

Seeing it again made me realize what a fool I'd been in my twenties. I, like Mickey and Eric now, had loved it. The raw feel, the sense of justice battered then fulfilled, especially by Sylvester Stallone with his vulnerability mixed with brutality. I hated the sheriff with a passion all out of proportion to his acting, and I still remembered the wash of pure joy I experienced when Galt fell from the helicopter. Now I saw the way my emotions had been manipulated, but then? I bought right into it.

Last night's dinner took place in a café down the street from our motel, a place Mickey swore he recognized from the movie, and which sported place mats pointing out local attractions. Mickey had carefully folded his up before any food or drink despoiled its pristine condition and now pulled it from his pocket. He studied it for a moment.

"Turn left here," he said, "then right at the stop sign."

Willing to be swept along, out of myself, I followed Mickey's directions. He bounced in the seat, the excitement spilling over to me, and I tried to remember being twelve. I had worked hard at being blasé by that time, pretending nothing and no one could interest or excite me. But I was getting interested now, and I didn't even like the movie.

I had forced myself to watch it once with Eric and Mickey, flinching at the blood, the broken bodies lying disregarded and forgotten on the ground. But somehow it still held me enthralled, for when I turned at the stop sign and pulled over, I imagined for a minute I saw Rambo on the bridge. Mickey echoed my sigh of contentment.

"It's really here," he said.

He stepped out of the car onto the gravel. The mountains rose around him, grave and stately, their peaks wrapped in mist, as he walked onto the bridge. I scrambled in my bag for the camera but didn't raise it to my face.

Mickey's back radiated not just surprise at finding art's reflection in the real world, but joy, as if he understood something that had long eluded him. I waited in the car,

Eric's filtered-through-his-earphones music in my head, watching Mickey walk across the bridge and back.

He slowed both ways as he reached the center, and stood, looking down into the water below. On the way back, he flexed his shoulders and struck a fighting stance. I watched in awe as he transformed himself from a skinny twelve-year-old computer nerd into Rambo, macho man of action. I didn't even have to imagine the camouflage pants and machine gun; Mickey had it all. He stood for a moment, Rambo shining from every pore, and then he grinned, himself again. He raced back to the car, map flapping, and threw himself into the front seat.

"Okay," he said, "go across the bridge and up the hill. We'll go to the Quintette—" he looked at me, not questioning our destination, only his pronunciation, "—Tunnels. Did you bring a flashlight? The map says we'll need one."

I nodded. I had packed three flashlights, although I suspected they were buried somewhere deep in the trunk. Mickey's faith in the map was complete, but I thought we could probably get away without artificial lighting on this bright summer day. Mickey's cheerful voice chattered on, reading from the map, telling me where to turn and what I looked at, locations from the movie, mostly, and I recognized them all, the scenery baked right into my brain.

Seeing it again brought back a year of my life I had successfully forgotten until now.

I was back in Vancouver. Susan and I were friends, best friends, though neither of us admitted it. I came home planning to take the summer off, a reward for putting myself through school. I spent one week living in my mother's most recent attempt at a home, long enough to realize I couldn't stand it, and started job hunting, determined to take the first one offered. I had enough money for one month's rent and food and a desperation to get out of my mother's house. The bank was my way out. I assured myself it was a temporary job, but the money and freedom went to my head.

I partied and drank too much, woke up too many mornings looking up at cracks on ceilings I didn't recognize. I met Dennis at the Saint Regis, slumming one Friday night with a bunch of people from work. An aura of confidence surrounded him. It was months before I saw it for what it was—the layer of alcohol he pickled himself in combined with the five beers I drank on an empty stomach.

We spent that weekend together and by Monday morning he had moved his few belongings into my small and exceedingly messy apartment. I arrived home from work to a new world, one in which starched and ironed white shirts lived on blue metal hangers, jackets on wooden ones, socks and underwear were folded and placed just so. I'd never lived with a man before except my father (an army man), so I took this as normal behavior. The possessiveness and anger, too.

I learned quickly I was deficient in most ways, and learned almost as quickly to blame my mother for it. That's what Dennis did. I also learned to lie about who I saw and when. I met Susan for lunch almost every day, telling Dennis I ate, by myself, in the food fair in the basement of the mall. He told me I had a lot to learn before I'd make a good wife and I believed him. I did the dishes wrong, I didn't have any idea of how to make a bed, and as for tuna salad… I was a disaster.

But Dennis knew what to do. He knew how I should dress and act. He taught me to cook and clean and shop. We never spent a penny we didn't need to except on alcohol and cigarettes for him, because he needed them after a hard day's work. I dieted. Dennis sent me off to work with carrots, celery sticks and a no-name brand diet shake, which I threw away as I got off the bus.

Susan bought me lunch—I had no spending money—great bags of French fries; fat, greasy hamburgers or fish and chips; strawberry shakes and chocolate-chip cookies. No wonder the scale went up rather than down. No wonder Dennis started feeding me dressingless salads and diet pills for dinner. No wonder I felt I couldn't cope, as if Dennis were the only thing standing between me and a complete breakdown. No wonder I said yes when he asked me to marry him.

"He'll look after me," I said to Susan the next day, showing off the minuscule diamond on my left hand. "He knows everything. I'll never make a mistake with Dennis around."

The look on Susan's face was bitter enough to curdle milk, but she said nothing about my engagement.

"Stop taking those diet pills, Randy. Look what they're doing to you." She grabbed my hand and held it out, until the shaking became obvious even to me. "Look at yourself." She turned my head toward the mirrored column next to us. She touched the bags under my eyes, the lank stringy hair on my forehead, the loose white skin on my arms, the permanent tic on my cheek.

"Those pills are killing you. Stop taking them."

Her face was more serious than I'd ever seen it, her eyes, so like mine, steady and clear. She looked scared. I raised my hand to catch the glitter of the diamond and watched it shake. I held on with my other hand to stop the tremor. I couldn't. It was permanent, as was the tic under my right eye and the feeling of incipient nausea. I turned away from the mirror, unable to face my ruined self, turned back to the frightened, determined face of my sister. I nodded.

The lying I had learned stood me in good stead when I got home that night.

"Did you take your pill?" Dennis asked in passing.

"Uh-huh," I said as I dropped it down the sink while I rinsed the dishes after dinner. Pork chops, baked potatoes, creamed corn for him, tomato and cucumbers for me. It was necessary to rinse the dishes in boiling water before washing them in more boiling water. I wore two pairs of rubber gloves—any more and I couldn't feel what I was doing and started breaking things—and my hands still looked and felt like boiled lobsters.

But I felt better the next day, more like my old self, and even better the day after that. It took a week for the shaking to stop and another month for me to figure out a way to leave. I waited for Dennis to drive by on his way to work and then went back into the apartment for my clothes.

I left everything except my personal belongings. I threw them into boxes, cramming things in all higgledy-piggledy, clothes and shoes and photographs and ornaments and records and books piled in grocery-store boxes. No order, just panic. I left my engagement ring in the exact center of the perfect French-polished table. I left no note, no word of goodbye. What could I say?

Forgive me, I was stupid to have imagined myself in love with you? Or, *Goodbye, Dennis, go ahead and kill yourself?* There was nothing to say.

He knew where I was. Susan's phone rang almost constantly for three weeks before falling ominously silent.

"I'll kill myself if you don't marry me," he'd said on the day he proposed. I thought at the time that he didn't know how to tell me he loved me, couldn't say those words. I saw the threat as a declaration of sorts, a way of saying it without having to say it. Now I wondered if he'd been telling the truth. I watched the local news, read the papers, called his office with my voice disguised, every single day to make sure he lived.

"Of course he won't kill himself. Just trying to keep you in line, that's all. And it worked for a while, didn't it?" Susan's acerbic voice kept me from going back.

The Quintette Tunnels didn't appear in First Blood or, if they did, they were well enough disguised that I didn't recognize them. I needed no more reminders of Dennis and the last time my life had been totally out of control. Coping with the present—unemployed, my sister sick, and me on the road trip from hell with two unhappy teenage boys—was enough. More than enough.

We wandered down the gravel path to the tunnels, the smell of the mountains strong in my nostrils. I tried to classify it, a smell different from anywhere else in the world. No sea salt, no desert-dry dust, nothing cultivated. It was a wild combination of damp, decaying plant life, cool lichen-draped rock, a faint undercurrent of some sweet-smelling wildflower, all of it overlaid with pine and cedar and fir. I heard the river in the background and thought maybe the smell of the river was part of it, the part I couldn't identify.

We turned a corner and there they were, cut off from their purpose, railway tracks and tunnels leading nowhere, an attraction for tourists, a destination rather than a journey.

The boys raced ahead of me, Eric taking one step to every two of Mickey's. One minute they were silhouetted in the daylight against the black of the tunnel, then vanished, leaving a weak image behind, like the sun on the inside of your eyelids after you closed them, like the unreliable memory of an old boyfriend, there but no longer accessible.

I followed them into the darkness, my mind still somewhere else: on Dennis, on the unique scent of mountain, on the odd feel of unseen gravel beneath my feet. With one part of my mind I worried about tripping over a rail or a rock or even a dead body left over from the movie, while the rest of me concentrated on the blackness. Darker than any night in the city, the tunnel wrapped me in its lightless embrace, chilling me right through my sweater.

I shivered and stopped, feeling as if I'd lost my hearing along with the light. I strained to hear the crunch of gravel, scared to move in case I really had gone deaf and could no longer hear my footsteps. The thump-thump of my heart, far from being reassuringly ordinary, beat too hard, as if it, too, wished to escape. The silence and the darkness were cold and absolute. Time passed without measurement. One minute or an hour. It might have been either to my paralyzed brain.

"Oooooooooooo, oooooooooo." The ghostly sound was immediately followed by the comforting ring of Mickey's giggle, snapping me from my paralysis. Two steps and a turn took me into a kind of gray twilight, another two into daylight.

The boys waited for me on a trestle bridge over a gorge complete with a raging roar of water, racing to get through the canyon into the peaceful eddies of the river beyond. Instead of utter silence, my ears filled with sound, the water's white noise a counterpoint to Mickey's laugh and the shrill whistle of a bird in the bushes growing out of the rock beside me. I had traveled from death into life, and the relief overwhelmed me.

The bridge trembled beneath my feet; the movement magnified under my hands on the railing as Eric bounced on the tracks. I watched the water swirl through the gorge, lost in its power and beauty until the spray from the river cooled my face and I shivered and gathered up the boys for the trip back to the car.

"The Hope Slide is just up the road," Mickey said as we settled into our familiar places. "It took down the whole side of a mountain. People are still buried under it. They never found them. Cool, huh?" The excitement in his voice made me smile. "Do you think if we dig, we'll find a skeleton? Maybe just a dog or a cat or something."

I glanced back at Eric. He had the palest of smiles on his face and his permanently attached earphones dangled from his neck. No tinny sounds, just the faint smile.

Maybe the journey would be fine, maybe I could change my biorhythms and learn, finally, to sleep like I never did as a teenager, long and slow and deep. I grinned at the thought. My mother would have killed me if I slept past eight, and here I was, contemplating sleeping until noon. Maybe it was time.

Eric's Notebook

I hate this. But I can't open my mouth 'cause I'll say it all, everything. If I start talking I won't be able to stop. So I don't. I say yes and no, a few words to Mum, but mostly I just listen to my music and try to draw.

There's lots to draw and we're always stopping so I have time. But nothing works out. It sucks big time. It's been three days and we've hardly got anywhere. We'll never get to Cranberry Portage let alone home again. I don't care.

Mum doesn't need me, she said so. And Mickey and Randy are happy, always talking, and stopping to look at one damn thing after another. They drive me crazy—how can they be so cheerful?

Mum's at home, dying. We're trapped in

this car going nowhere. I never a get a minute to myself. Not one single minute. Only in the bathroom and even then I can hear them waiting for me, listening, always listening. I want to go home. Right now. If we turn around…

If we turn around we'll be home in a couple of days. I bet we'll go faster home than away. But no one else cares. Only me.

CHAPTER 4

Dragonflies always know which way is up and use body positioning to regulate their temperature. In the extreme heat of summer, dragonflies can orientate themselves so their heads are down, away from the sun, and the tip of their abdomen is pointed at the sun. The "obelisk" position is used to shade the thorax.
—*The Sunshine Coast News*, September 14, 2005

We soon established a routine—up and at 'em at the crack of noon. We managed it that early only because of checkout times. Our average forward movement over the first five days was less than two hours of driving a day, 150 kilometers, more or less. When I said forward motion, I meant away from home because, of course, we clocked many more miles than those in a direct line from home to our ultimate destination. I expected us to be halfway across the prairies by now; instead, we were mired in the Rockies and showed no signs of breaking out. My trip odometer showed we'd traveled almost 1500 kilometers, putting us, on the map, some-where around Swift Current in the middle of Sas-katchewan. We were still in the same damn time zone, on the British Columbia side of the Rockies, two provinces away from where we should be, and less than 650 kilometers away from where we started.

Mickey appointed himself chief tour guide and route planner, and locked us into the mountains until I felt like a very stupid rat in a maze or a silver marble in a pinball machine, bouncing from bumper to bumper.

There wasn't a museum of any kind he didn't want to stop at—gold mining, farming, ranching, pioneer—we saw them all. We waited until an old man (occasion-ally an old woman) pulled into the gravel parking lot in a perfectly preserved thirty-year-old Ford half an hour after the scheduled opening time. He or she fum-bled for five minutes with the key to the door and then all of us, including the docent, spent the next thirty minutes dutifully shuffling from one dusty exhibit to the next. It didn't take long to become experts on gold panning, early farm implements, the Hudson's Bay Company, policing in the mountains in the nineteenth century, and numerous other obscure facets of the his-tory of whatever town we were in at the time.

We hiked up unmarked trails hunting for faded pic-tographs and most times didn't find them. I figured it was the only exercise—except for the museum shuffle—we were getting, so what could it hurt?

"Follow me," Mickey called from around a corner of the barely visible trail. "They're up here. I know they are." He'd been saying those exact words for days, and I no longer questioned them, just carried on up the trail behind him.

Eric put on a burst of speed, his long legs and Mickey's enthusiasm placing me squarely in the back of the pack, and also disappeared around the corner. At first, I found the silence unsettling, but then it started. Tiny rattlings in the bushes, birds singing, the wind whispering sweet nothings to the trees. I unkinked my shoulders, took a deep breath of the fragrant air and followed the boys up the slope.

The path curved around and, with a suddenness that shocked me, turned into an enchanted forest. The boys stood enthralled in the middle of it. Bright green moss carpeted the ground, stifling all sound except the sweet whistles of an unseen songbird. The trees opened up into this clearing, bowing away from the center like an orchestra around a conductor, leaving room for the sun to shoot through in precisely formed rays of light. Unconsciously, the boys had placed themselves directly in the sun, their hair and faces shining, looking for all the world like saints in some Renaissance painting. I stood at the edge of the clearing, my camera to my eye, and made a wish that I might somehow capture this moment for Susan, wishing too that she could be here with us. I snapped a picture, breaking the spell for all of us.

Mickey ran out of the clearing, Eric at his heels. That struck me as odd. I'd never, until today, seen Eric behind Mickey. He was the leader, big brother, hero. Yet, now that I noticed it, I realized, at least for these past couple of weeks, that was no longer true. Along with his voice, Eric had abandoned his role as big brother.

The pictographs, straight up another hour, followed by fifteen uncomfortable minutes scrambling up a scree slope, were worth the effort. A large rock stood at the top of the slope as if a giant had surveyed the mountaintop and then carefully placed it in this exact spot for maximum effect. The faint red marks on the dark gray suggested rust or blood from a distance but close up the pictures revealed themselves.

Elk and grizzly, fish and birds, squirrels, even chipmunks, each with their own distinct outline and place in the ordered world of the long-dead artist. I walked around the rock, my fingertips aching to touch the perfect dragonfly centered on its back, but scared to contribute to its fading. How many years had this paint survived the extremes of the mountain weather? Blizzards, rainstorms, blistering heat. Yet it lingered on, a faint memory, perhaps, of its earlier self, but more than sufficient to capture my imagination.

"These drawings are hundreds of years old," Mickey said, reading from his guidebook. "Can you believe that? Maybe they repaint them every summer, like we do our fence."

Interest waning, he scurried down the scree slope to the small lake at the bottom and started searching for stones to skip. I sat on a smaller rock, one safely embedded in the slope, girding myself for the trip down. I hated scree slope. Going up was barely okay, going down awful. I hated the feel of the loose rock under my feet, never did get the hang of the skating motion essential for safe passage, so I usually ended up spending half my time sliding down, out of control, and the other half on my butt.

Eric stood in the shadow of the big rock, a piece of red drawing chalk in his hand, scribbling feverishly in the sketch pad he had pulled from his backpack. His fingers moved with a confidence far beyond his years and I saw the man he would become. I saw Susan in the intensity of his concentration, the tilt of his head, the shape of his face. Nothing of Don, at least that I could see, although maybe the sullenness came from his father. Susan got angry loudly, never silently.

I didn't ever know Don that well. He was good at erecting walls between himself and others—a friendly, slightly distant, impenetrable facade—the real man rarely exposed. For the first time, I wondered if he had ever exposed himself to Susan, or the boys, but when I thought about it for a while, I continued to doubt it.

Every day, we called home three times and with each phone call Susan sounded better. All of us memorized my calling card number and quickly established a system. Mickey made the first call, usually from the motel just before we checked out. This varied only if we didn't have a phone in the room, which happened, as we got farther into the mountains and deeper into my savings, more often than not. Then his call was from wherever we had breakfast. He told us the news while we ate, our plates piled increasingly higher as we moved away from the coast.

We watched for cafés with hand-lettered signs proclaiming *All Day Breakfast Special*—$2.99. Bacon, three eggs, sausage, hash browns, pancakes and toast. The waitresses cheerfully complied with our requests for refills on the syrup.

I didn't have the courage (or Eric the voice) to ask Mickey about Susan, so breakfast remained silent until Mickey arranged his cutlery, the glasses of juice and ice water, and the various sticky jars of syrup and jam (no miniature sanitized square packets here). Once everything was placed to his satisfaction, he talked.

"The roses are blooming and she cut some of those

big red ones for the house. They smell great but she has to water them twice a day. The sun hasn't stopped shining since we left."

An almost imperceptible grimace crossed his face as we contemplated the rare coastal sunshine and Susan relaxing on the porch.

"The nurse comes by to change the bandages and the rest of the time she's just hanging around. I bet she's getting a great suntan."

I tried to decipher her health from these clues. She was well enough to go outside, pick roses and water them. I took comfort from this evidence of normality. Susan loved her roses, pampered them in a way she did nothing else.

Eric's call to Susan took place as the long twilight began, hours earlier than on the Coast. The mountains cut off direct sunlight early in the evening, shadows stretching over the valleys with disconcerting haste. Used to the leisurely summer sunsets on the Coast, I was often caught unaware by the swift onset of darkness and the absence of streetlights. I drove more by feel than by sight. Turning on the headlights became the signal to hunt for a phone booth. Mickey and I pretended not to watch while Eric hunched over the phone, the receiver in his right hand, his left playing an invisible keyboard.

Mickey had none of the fear Eric and I displayed. Before Eric could put his earphones back on and shut us out, Mickey leaped in.

"What did she say?"

"She's fine" was Eric's standard reply.

"Did you tell her to feed the fish?"

"Nope."

"What about Jesse?" Jesse was Mickey's beloved turtle, who had grown from the size of a quarter until he now occupied a fifty-gallon aquarium in solitary splendor. No fish lived with him; they had their own, smaller space. It took five batches of guppies and neon tetras to discover Jesse's favorite food was fish.

"Nope."

Eric was barely visible in the back seat, but I didn't need to see him to know what he looked like. His expression never varied. In fact, for a moment, I wondered, alarmingly, whether he'd had a stroke. But his speech wasn't slurred and his whole face, not just half, was immobile, and he ate, and drew, as always, with both hands. So not a stroke but fear caused the rigidity to settle over his features.

I sneaked out of the room once the boys were asleep to make my call. I waited on my double bed while the boys carefully separated themselves on the other, practically falling off opposite sides. I strained to catch the sound of their breathing slow and soften into sleep until it was indistinguishable from the hum of trucks on the highway. I counted backward in the never-quite-dark rooms, starting at one thousand over and over again as I jerked myself awake, having lost track for the third or fourth or fifth time.

I stood in phone booths rattling in the slipstreams of the passing eighteen-wheelers, the hum raised to a roar, the volume on the phone turned as high as it would go, and listened to Susan recount her progress, and hid my yawns.

"I'm better today. Tired, but I walked around the block. The radiation starts in a couple of weeks, once the shunt and the stitches are out. Steve—" her surgeon "—says I'm doing better than anyone expected."

I told her only the good parts of the day, omitting the fights and the silences, entertaining her with my tale of a city girl trapped in the country.

"We went to a ghost town up the highway. All the houses were open and you could wander through them as if you were their neighbors or something. They had plates and glasses and stuff all over the tables, as if the people just got up and walked away, leaving everything behind. Gave me the creeps."

"Sounds like *Day of the Triffids*."

I remembered the summer I first read that book, the same summer Susan had. I was thirteen, Mum was working, and I was supposed to be looking after Susan. I was old enough, Mum said, and besides, she couldn't afford a babysitter because we were at the top end of our sliding housing scale. A couple of months before, we'd left behind the renovated chicken coop—cheap, but beginning to regurgitate the smell of the chickens in the warm spring—and moved into a three-bedroom bungalow with a half basement. I was used to the arc. We started at the top in a place slightly too expensive.

"We can afford it if we're careful. If we give up…"

The list of what we'd give up was endless and ever changing. Haircuts—she'd cut our hair herself; eating out—which we only ever did at McDonald's anyway; new clothes, she'd buy a secondhand sewing machine. None of that ever happened.

After three or four months, the rent check would bounce and we'd move somewhere a little cheaper, but still not quite cheap enough. And so on, over and over, until we ended up, yet again, in the equivalent of the chicken coop. She'd immediately start reading the rentals portion of the paper, drawing up long columns of figures, crossing out the things we (mostly me, it felt like) could do without, so we could move into another slightly too expensive but infinitely more desirable residence.

The year I turned thirteen and was a full-blown teenager, I planned to enjoy the summer, and that did not include spending any of my time watching my baby sister. Each morning, I handed her a list of chores, simple-but-time-consuming ones. Quiet ones. Polishing the silver. Dusting. Ironing. Defrosting the fridge. Cleaning the oven. She cheerfully accomplished them all and then sat playing in the backyard until lunch. We ate the same three things for lunch all summer. Kraft Dinner. Chef Boyardee ravioli. Peanut-butter-and-banana sandwiches.

Our new house was in a neighborhood just far enough from the chicken coop that I didn't see my friends from school. So my only companion was Roy Townsend, the son of a friend of my mother's who lived around the corner. He was a couple of years older than me and under normal circumstances (if circumstances could ever be said to be normal in my family), I wouldn't have had anything to do with him. Tall and skinny, lank, greasy hair, one eye wobbling behind heavy-framed glasses. He wore shapeless brown corduroys instead of jeans, and T-shirts bearing the names of bands I'd never heard of. But I was desperate and he was smart. Smarter than anyone else I knew.

I spent the summer reading the ragged paperbacks he lent me by the score and watching soap operas on the black-and-white television in the basement, hiding in the cool darkness from the heat of the afternoons. Susan joined me for the soaps, sitting on the chair across the room. We never spoke but we were partners in a conspiracy of silence against our mother and the life she forced us to live. We said nothing to her of the way we spent our days. As a reward for Susan's complicity, I passed Roy's books on to her and she read them in the flickering light of the television.

The Day of the Triffids was the first science-fiction book I'd ever read and its images of the death of the world were burned into my brain. I wasn't so much interested in its possible rebirth. Instead, I fixated on the empty cities, the free food and clothes in the deserted shops, the choice of desirable residences, with new furniture and no cleaning to do. All I needed to do, when the dust and dirt and dishes piled up, was move to another flat. It sounded like a perfect world and, despite the dozens of other books I read that summer, the empty streets of London stayed with me.

Twice that summer Roy and I went downtown and spent Saturday at the movies, returning home before the sun set. Those days were planned with military precision, requiring the aid of maps and schedules, so as to fit the maximum number of movies into the minimum time, and still be home in time for dinner. My mother's condition.

"Can we make it three blocks in five minutes?"

"What if we miss the previews?"

"How long, exactly, is the movie?"

I phoned and asked these kinds of questions. Roy had an aversion to the telephone, or maybe it was an aversion to work.

"Buy all the tickets before the first movie so we don't have to wait in line."

The planning took weeks but both Saturdays went without a hitch. We saw *High Plains Drifter*, *Conquest of the Planet of the Apes*, and *The Groundstar Conspiracy* one week; *The Poseidon Adventure*, *The Godfather*, and a repeat of *High Plains Drifter* the next. The only movie I remembered with any certainty was *The Poseidon Adventure*, because it scared me to death. I couldn't bear the thought of being trapped like that, knew I'd be one of the hysterical ones, left behind as a liability. I'd never be an asset. I knew it.

Roy and our mothers early on came to an agreement. He was too old for me, but he could see me in the daytime, although never during the week in my motherless house. I was pretty confident she had enlisted Susan as a spy, but confident enough Susan would say nothing, to invite Roy over for the afternoons, making sure he left the minute *General Hospital* was over, a full hour before my mother could get home, even if she left work right on time, which she never did.

That was the summer I learned about two kinds of lies—science fiction and love.

I read so much that the fiction part of the science fiction was easy to accept. I didn't really expect a perfect world, or a bomb to explode and leave a desert behind, or for man to travel to the stars, or for a comet to turn everyone blind. I'd spent years reading the always-changing and never diminishing piles of romances in Laundromats. And not one of those books bore the slightest resemblance to any reality I'd ever seen. So fiction, even my daydreams about *The Day of the Triffids*, was easily distinguished from real life.

It was different with Roy. I felt myself safe from him at the beginning. But he put in weeks of flattery, compliments the type of which I'd never had before. I was more used to comments about my breasts.

"You're smarter than you look."

"I love to talk to you."

"I can't believe you already finished that book. It took me twice as long. How did you learn to read so fast?"

That was easy. I'd spent my whole life—what I remembered of it, anyway—losing myself in books. And magazines. And the backs of cereal boxes. I read—devoured—anything and everything, and with Mum so busy with work and self-improvement, no one censored my reading. I read *Mandingo* and *Valley of the Dolls* before I had my first period. I knew stuff, all kinds of stuff, although none of it—even the hundreds of stories I'd read about lust and betrayal—helped me in this situation.

We'd sit in the basement, drapes drawn, a blanket over my bare legs, the room lit only by the television,

Susan's presence forgotten. Even now, almost thirty years later, I couldn't turn on the television in the afternoon without a flicker of excitement.

I'd watch the nurses and doctors, beautifully dressed, living in perfectly decorated homes. They saved lives, or lost them, fell in love or out, had affairs or got married. What I waited for was the inevitable moment when a man and a woman—married, engaged, someone else's spouse, casual acquaintances—started to kiss. That was what those shows were about for me. The hours of storyline, of intertwining relationships, came down to that first tentative meeting of the eyes, the careful steps forward, the touch of the hands.

And while I was engrossed in the escalating passion on the screen, Roy was engrossed in me. His hand started at my knee and moved slowly, surreptitiously, softly upward. He whispered in my ear, counterpoint to the moans of love on the television. He touched the bare skin at my waist, sending shivers through me. I heard the declarations of undying love on the television and ignored the declarations of overwhelming horniness from beside me.

Maybe ignored wasn't the best description. Confused? I believed Roy loved me and, with the greedy certitude of a thirteen-year-old, expected us to do as they did on the soaps. Go steady until we both graduated and then marry on the day I finished high school, all my classmates gathered around in an adoring bunch. A big wedding to show everyone what a wonderful girl I turned out to be. I even picked out my dress, choosing among the summer wedding fashions displayed on the soaps.

I hadn't thought as far ahead as September. I couldn't, not while he had his hands on me, not while I continued to confuse the on-screen passion with what was happening on my mother's second-hand couch.

The funny thing was I was sure, now, my mother knew what went on between Roy and me and ignored it, assuming my infatuation would disappear with the coming of fall and trusting Susan's presence to keep me, at least technically, a virgin. And she was right. It did.

The Labor Day weekend of 1972 was the first time I had my heart broken. Roy vanished into high school—I never saw him again, by the time I got there, he was gone—and I scuttled off to my first year of junior high.

Susan's voice brought me back to the diesel-scented air of the phone booth.

"Where are you?" she asked, and I looked up at the flickering neon sign above our motel.

"We're just outside of Nelson." The orange letters read Nelson Cottonwood Motel. "Maybe we'll spend the day there tomorrow. Or maybe we'll spend it at the lake. I think we need a break."

I respected Susan's restraint; she didn't say what I knew she thought.

A break? You're only a day away from home and it's taken you five days to get there. You've got to be joking.

But I couldn't tell Susan how exhausting it was, how I couldn't get back to sleep when I returned to the room after our phone calls, how I lay there, motionless in my bed, straining to hear the boys' breathing, desperate to distinguish one from the other. I couldn't tell her how I lay there as the sun came up, listening to the happy bustle of families getting on the road, how I sneaked out of my bed and sat on the grubby carpet next to the boys, put my head on the edge of their bed and waited, through the long morning hours, for them to stir. I couldn't tell her that, at the first sign of movement, I sprang from the floor and into the shower so they wouldn't know I'd been watching them.

I polished the city-mouse story in those conversations until it shone. I pulled anecdotes of people and places from every movie I'd ever seen, every book I'd ever read, changing them to fit my situation, hoping the boys wouldn't rat me out the next time they spoke to her. And sometimes, when the story I told went well, I almost believed it myself.

Eric's Notebook Two in the morning

I have dreams, bad ones, every night. I'm trapped in a sinking car, and everyone I know is standing on the edge of the ditch. They're watching me bang on the windows and doors but none of them move. And then they turn away and all I see are their backs. I hammer and yell—but there's no sound in my dream, like I'm wearing my earphones and the silence is cranked up as high as it can go. And nothing works. There are no handles. I can't break the windows.

And then I wake up. And I don't know where I am.

CHAPTER 5

Use a dark net (black or green) to collect dragonflies. They are more likely to see and evade a
white net. Do not wave the net around and swing
from behind as they pass by; dragonflies are very
quick and can dodge a net swung directly at them.
—*The Sunshine Coast News*, September 14, 2005

Cocooned in a bowl of mountains on the shore of a
deep, cold lake, Nelson reminded me of a miniature
Christmas village, the kind the perfect family built on
their hallway table for the holidays. Victorian houses
festooned with gingerbread and holly and exactly the
right amount of snow, not too much to obscure the exquisite shapes and colors, just enough to emphasize the
outlines. The trees of my village bore the mark of a full-
time gardener and were dusted with snow.

The square, surrounded by old-fashioned book and
toy and candy stores, sported a skating rink, its mirrored
surface reflecting the bright clothes and shining faces

of the children. This perfection scared me, felt too much like my mother's vision of Cranberry Portage. I wondered whether I'd been one of the brightly clad children, because I couldn't think of where that image came from, otherwise. Skating on a frozen pond? With my father?

I hoped this trip wasn't going to turn out to be an exhumation of my buried childhood. It was tough enough without that. I shook off the almost-memory of my father and turned my attention back to Nelson.

Like my mother's stories of Cranberry Portage, Nelson was almost too good to be true. I searched for the worm in the apple, the dark underbelly of the little town, but I didn't find it.

We wandered the streets, moving from craft store to café to coffee shop, never once encountering real life, at least the life I knew. No panhandlers, no drunks, no junkies, no rats scuttling across filth-infested alleys. No recently released mental patients mumbling to themselves on the buses or yelling at some invisible God or alien. No shuffling derelicts, no boarded-up stores, no rain. Nelson felt like a storybook world, a fantasy or a fairy tale. I kept expecting the wicked witch to appear. Or the beautiful princess. Or a dwarf. A goblin. An elf.

The boys took it all at face value, mostly happy to be out of the car and, like sailors after a long trip, enjoying the feel of solid ground beneath their feet. Even

Eric's sullen face brightened at the cheerful surroundings. He didn't smile, but at least he didn't look on the verge of tears. I was the cranky one. We arrived outside a window full of books and a sign offering tea and cookies. I drooled. I handed Eric and Mickey each a twenty-dollar bill.

"I'm staying here. You guys go do whatever. Stay together." I glanced at my watch. "It's three o'clock now. Be back at five-thirty and we'll have dinner."

Identical looks crossed their faces, compounded of relief at getting away from their bitchy aunt, fear at being alone in a strange place, and joy at the thought of how many video games twenty dollars would buy. I laughed to myself as the expressions chased each other, looking like the sing-along words scrolling across an old-fashioned movie screen. All that was missing was the bouncing red ball.

I stood in front of the store and watched the two of them head down the street until they turned at the corner—the short dark one skipping to some internal music, the tall blond one loping, his shoulders hunched against a ferocious wind felt only by one lonely, unhappy fifteen-year-old. I thought of Pigpen trailing a cloud of dirt. Eric's unhappiness was equally obvious and far more onerous. I shrugged my shoulders and opened the door of the bookstore. There was nothing I could do about Eric. I'd had plenty of sleepless nights to come up with a solution, and there wasn't one.

A bell rang somewhere in the depths of the shop as I stepped inside. I stopped, seduced on all fronts. The smells of paper and leather, coffee and chocolate, the sun warming the ceiling-high rows of books, picking out a few favorites with delicate shafts of light, the dust motes dancing in the aisles. Mozart overlaid with soft, relaxed conversations. The wooden floor creaked beneath my feet, bouncing at each step with a life of its own. I ran my hand along the row of books closest to me and sighed in contentment. I was home. Safe.

I closed my eyes in front of each of the poetry, fantasy, modern, and classic fiction sections and grabbed books at random. The tables in the coffee shop were empty. Without reading the titles, I placed my books on the table farthest from the window. I didn't want to look out at the storybook village filled with storybook people. I wanted to imagine myself somewhere else. Not hundreds of kilometers away from home and Susan. Not trapped in a small white car smelling of teenage boy and greasy fried food. Not locked in pine-coated mountains without a hint of salt or sea spray. At the back table, maybe I could pretend I was at home.

Earl Grey tea with lemon and a nanaimo bar was my afternoon snack of choice. I thought of the look Susan would give me if she saw me with my back to the shop.

She joked about my insistence on the back row at movies and concerts, my maneuvering for the seat facing out at restaurants. I hated having people behind me.

All my rooms, without conscious planning on my part, followed the principles of feng shui. I never sat or stood with my back to the door. I was a natural gunslinger. But today the itching on the back of my neck was a small price to pay for a couple of hours of oblivion.

The scent of bergamot and lemon wafted up from the rose-covered teacup, sending me back twenty years to the day I arrived in England and met my Auntie Mabel.

My father's life was a romantic story to me, learning it in the town where he'd been born, in a house filled with memories of a generation of lost men. My father, Ben, had been sent, along with hundreds of other kids, across the ocean to stay with elderly, distant relations in Toronto, safe from the ravages of war. He never went back.

His three older brothers died in the war, one at El Alamein, one in a prison camp in Germany, the other somewhere on the North Sea. None of their bodies made it back to Reigate, including my father's. I knew none of this story until the summer I met Auntie Mabel, the sole survivor of five children.

The flight wasn't much longer than the one I'd taken from Vancouver to Toronto, the biggest difference being the accents and uniforms of the attendants. I landed at Gatwick, took the train into Victoria Station and right back out again to Reigate. In less than twelve hours I had traveled 5,700 kilometers and fifty years into the past.

Mabel met me at the station. A taxi waited with her, the kind you saw in old movies, big and black and unwieldy on the half-size roads. A five-minute drive and we were walking in the front gate of 27 Red Court Lane, the house where my father, his father and grandfather, had been born in the small room on the right at the top of the steep stairway. We manhandled my suitcase around the tight corners and up the steps. I was to sleep in the room on the left.

"The boys all slept here," she said. "I always had my own room," she continued, a trace of pride in her voice. "I'll show you round the rest of the house after tea. The loo's at the back." She pointed out the window to a small wooden structure nestled against the fence at the end of the garden.

"Come down when you're ready. I'll just pop the kettle on."

That first afternoon stayed with me as if it were a movie I'd seen a thousand times. Even today, I remembered every single detail, the exact inflection of her shaky old voice, the moment the sun began to fall beneath the steep roofs of the houses across the lane. The cup I held in my hand in the coffee shop in Nelson was no more real to me than the Royal Albert roses I drank from at Auntie Mabel's twenty years ago.

She told me about Ben in one long continuous rush, a single take. She'd been rehearsing the story since the day I was born, I thought, or at least since the day she received the card and photo prominently displayed on the wall above the fireplace. My father's handwriting was firm and old-fashioned as he told his sister about the birth of his daughter—Miranda Jane Roman. Me. The writing looked familiar although I knew I'd never seen it before. My mother often lamented the fact she had no more of his writing than his signature on their marriage certificate.

"That's my name, you know. Jane is my middle name. After my grandmother. Your great-grandmother." Her finger caressed the faded ink. "Ben was a sweet boy and he grew into a sweet man. I know he did, even though I never saw him again. Every year he sent me packages at Christmas and Easter and for my birthday. And long letters about you girls. I kept them all."

Until I sat in her kitchen on that sunny afternoon, I hadn't really figured out who the woman sending Christmas cards and English books for birthdays truly was. My father's sister, someone who grew up with him, someone who knew him before my mother met him and turned him into an impossible hero.

"Ben was the baby. First Fred, then Harry and Don,

then me, then Ben. We were closest in age, less than a year apart, so we went everywhere together. Mother kept me back a year so we could be in the same form at school. Everyone thought we were twins." She smiled at the thought and I imagined her and Ben pretending to everyone they were twins, enjoying the joke.

She handed me a photograph of two children in school uniforms. She was right—they looked enough alike to be twins. Same height and build, same hair and eyes—all of which I'd inherited.

"We were never apart for a single day until we got evacuated. The older boys were already in the army or waiting to get in, so it was only Ben and me. And they had to split us up, boys one place, girls another. I never saw Ben again. They sent him to Canada after Mother and Father died. I stayed on and helped in the house where I was billeted. But he wrote me every week without fail until he died. And I wrote him. I kept all his letters, every one of them.

"Ben loved you, Miranda, more than anything, I think. He wrote pages and pages about your first smile, your baby teeth, your first steps. He sent me an airmail letter just to tell me when you spoke your first word. Dada. He was so proud of you and I was so happy for him. He wanted to bring you for a visit, but your mother was scared to fly."

My mother? Bullshit. She spent half her life on the

plane to Reno. But I couldn't tell Mabel that. My trip to England sealed the rift between my mother and I. She wanted Ben all to herself, wanted the memory of him to be hers alone. No Mabel, no past, certainly no fatherhood. Her stories were of the romantic love they shared, the photographs she kept were of the two of them together. Sitting at Mabel's kitchen table, I saw for the first time pictures of my father holding me, his love obvious in the tender way he cradled my head, the soft smile on his face. I never forgave my mother for not telling me he loved me as much as her.

The coffee shop emptied around me as people left to return to work or home or shopping. I refilled my teapot twice before I got around to checking the titles of the books I'd picked at random. An anthology of British war poetry, compiled to celebrate the fiftieth anniversary of the end of the war. *The Hobbit*, which I'd read as a teenager and not since. *Huckleberry Finn*, which I'd never read because I didn't like *Tom Sawyer*, and *Bridges of Madison County*, which I hated.

I put back the last and paid for the rest. My optimistic thought was that the poetry would be good to read while the boys made yet another pit stop. The others I would read in the evenings and in the pale light of the long mornings beside the boys' bed. The books I'd packed, all new and unknown, turned out to be too risky. I absolutely could not read anything with a sad ending. If I once started to cry I wouldn't be able to stop.

From that thought, it was only a step to picturing myself traveling across the country, watching the highway through a veil of hot tears, sleeping (or not) on soggy pillows, stopping two or three times a day for another box of Kleenex, leaving a trail of damp tissues behind me. The boys would be embarrassed and uncomfortable—an understatement—and an already bad situation would get infinitely worse. Books I knew, books with happy endings—cozy mysteries, fantasies, classics—those were the ticket.

The shop hummed along behind my back. The boys would arrive any minute. They were conscientious about deadlines, seldom more than fifteen minutes late, although they tended to push for those fifteen minutes. My watch said 5:45 p.m. when a shadow crossed my table. Eric.

"Where's Mickey?" I wasn't worried; he loved bookstores almost as much as I did and I'd noticed a huge nature section at the back. Mickey's favorite kind of book had some huge blowup of a bug or a tick or a dust mite on the cover. A monster created from something invisible.

"He's not here?" Eric's voice squeaked a little as he asked the question.

"I haven't seen him. He's not with you?" I looked

around the restaurant, expecting to see his dark head at the counter. After all, he hadn't eaten for almost three hours. Neither of them was likely to use their money for food. But there was no Mickey and when I looked back up at Eric, I started to worry. His usually ruddy face had turned as pale as Mickey's.

"Where'd you see him last?"

"At the video arcade. He was playing some bug game."

That was more than Eric had spoken in my presence in weeks but I was too worried about Mickey to appreciate it.

"And?"

"That's it. I was playing a VR game and when I turned around, he was gone. I went right through the place. And around the block. Didn't find him."

He waited for me to tell him what to do. I surprised myself.

"Sit." I pulled out the chair beside mine. "I'll get you a drink and a bun. He'll show up. He's only a few minutes late."

Eric's slumped shoulders straightened the slightest bit. He ostentatiously took off his watch and placed it on the table in front of him as if to say, *okay, I'll give you a few minutes to be right, but only a few, before I start to panic again.*

I knew exactly how he felt. My panic was just below the surface, digging its claws into the walls of the well, dragging its way up the slimy cold bricks. It wouldn't be long before it popped its head up into the sunlight. I kicked it back down into the water at the bottom while I ordered a root beer and an apple fritter for Eric. That gave me a few more minutes before it made it back up to the surface.

Neither of us spoke while Eric ate and drank as if he hadn't done either for days. When he was finished, he calmly picked up his watch, fastened it to his wrist, and untangled himself and his backpack from the chair.

"I'm going to look for him. He must have got turned around. He's never late. Not like this."

"Okay. I'll come too. But let's pick a meeting place and time because he'll probably come back here and start to worry when we're not here."

Eric's feet tapped on the wooden floor while he waited for my instructions.

"Back here in half an hour, okay? Don't go too far. Mickey wouldn't. Besides, the town's not that big."

He nodded and stomped out the door. I followed. He turned left, away from the video arcade. I turned right. I didn't want to believe Mickey was lost. He read a map better than anyone I knew and he had an unerring sense of direction. But Eric's concern transmitted itself to me and I raced through the streets, scanning the late afternoon crowds for Mickey's sleek dark head. Nothing. Blocks and blocks and blocks of nothing. The arcade, when I got there, was full of kids, yelling and shrieking and giggling, creating an unbearable din that I tried, without success, to ignore.

The noise escalated my anxiety into panic. I ran from room to room, my eyes hurrying ahead of me, my heart and lungs aching with fear. Still no Mickey.

The streets were darker when I left the arcade, darker and emptier. The many restaurants turned on their lights as I passed, spilling life onto the streets. I scurried into dark alleys, my throat sore from calling Mickey's name. Time passed in the oddest way—quickly, my half hour was long up, and interminably, each street miles long.

The trip back to the bookstore took forever, my steps slowing with each block. I didn't want to turn the corner. How could I tell Susan?

Eric stood in the doorway, his back to me. I cringed. He leaned against the wall as if it were all that was holding him up. His posture looked familiar, although when I placed it I was sorry I had. He leaned against that wall in the way I'd seen search-and-rescue workers lean against their trucks or tree trunks when they'd failed to save the snowboarder skiing out of bounds, or the hiker who disappeared and spent the night on the mountain, or the child trapped by a fire in a third-floor bedroom. The stance spoke of exhaustion and despair and regret. Eric hadn't found Mickey, either.

I knew it. The whole circus surrounding his kidnapping or running away or being in a car accident, the police, social workers, the search teams and dogs, the media, sprang into full bloom before my eyes.

But before all that happened, I had to deal with Eric. He needed me.

"Eric?" I touched his shoulder.

"We have to go to the police. I saw the station. It's just around the corner," Eric spoke, his voice flat and certain.

His face fell in on itself. I knew what he'd been thinking as he waited for me because I'd been thinking it, too. We'd get back to the bookstore and Mickey would be pacing outside, waiting for us, and pissed off because we weren't where we said we'd be. He'd be hungry so the first thing we would do, after we yelled at him for being late, would be to walk down the street to the coffee shop at the corner. We'd order grilled-cheese sandwiches, fries, chocolate milk and Mickey would tell us how he found a secret tree house, a bee-hive, or a store full of bugs.

Instead, I touched Eric's shoulder again and headed for the police station. We had three hours before I'd have to tell Susan I lost her son. My steps quickened. I felt the sweat darken my clothes, smelled it as I hurried down the street. It was fear-sweat, clear and rank. Heads turned as I passed, their attention caught, their stomachs churning as they smelled it. Panic. And they turned away. Ignored me and hoped they'd never smell it again.

The station was a small gray stone building. The size of it gave me hope. No serious crimes could be expected. The woman at the front desk rose and came out from behind her barrier before I said a word.

"What's happened?" she asked, her hands reaching for me.

Eric told her the story while I sat hyperventilating on a polished wooden chair. He produced a photo of Mickey from his wallet, carefully pointing out the differences: in Mickey's haircut, his T-shirt, his faint suntan.

"He's just got turned around," the woman said. "It happens all the time with kids. Adults, too. It's because the mountains are all around. There's no frame of reference."

What she said made sense to me, gave me comfort. Because that was how I felt the whole time I lived in Toronto. Lost on the flat plain of that city, directionless. Even after five years I continued to look up, expecting to see the mountains, to have them tell me which way was which. And each time they weren't there I felt physically ill, as if the world I knew had vanished and I had been dumped into a parallel universe.

"Go back to the bookstore. We'll look for—" she glanced at the report on her desk for his name

"—Mickey, but he'll probably find you before we find him. Don't worry. He'll be fine."

She sounded so much like Susan, so confident, so sure of herself. I wanted to believe her, I really did. But I couldn't. I knew what had happened.

A gang of bikers—we'd seen plenty of them on our way through the mountains—had kidnapped Mickey to use him as a sex slave. It would have been easy. Mickey loved motorcycles, second only to bugs. I'd have to phone Susan in—I checked my watch to find we'd only been in the police station for forty-five minutes although it felt like forever—in exactly 135 minutes. I couldn't breathe. She'd never forgive me. I'd never forgive myself.

Careless wasn't the word for it. Stupid. Selfish. Inconsiderate. Totally unacceptable behavior.

Eric had outpaced me and stood, again, in the doorway of the bookstore. While I watched, the streetlights turned on around him, catching his eyes and white-blond head. He looked tired in a way no teenager should, tired through to his bones, long-term deep exhaustion. That was my fault, too.

Then he turned toward me and smiled his old, big smile for the first time in weeks. Mickey sat on the pavement at his feet, a puppy cradled on his lap. And after all that, how could I say no to Dexter? He already had a name and he made Eric smile. Besides, we couldn't travel any slower. I tried to ignore the problems I knew would come from traveling with an untrained puppy and concentrated instead on the joy in the three faces in front of me.

"Time to find a room. And a pet store. And tomorrow, a vet. We need to make sure Dexter's healthy and has had his shots. And we need to buy a leash and food and…"

Another day in Nelson. Another day behind schedule. But we'd have a chance to go to the Ukrainian restaurant I'd spotted in my search for Mickey and have perogies for breakfast. It wasn't all bad.

CHAPTER 6

As the wetlands disappear, the food supply for
dragonflies is becoming scarcer. As food dimin-
ishes, dragonflies may grow more slowly, even ab-
normally, become diseased or die.
—*The Sunshine Coast News*, September 14, 2005

Dexter changed things, the most obvious being that
Mickey got over his lifelong aversion to the back seat.
He listened to my decree that Dexter wasn't allowed in
the front, and he chose to sit in the back, leaving Eric
next to me. The dimensions in the car altered, becoming smaller, more claustrophobic. Eric used up all the
air in the front seat so I drove, day and night, with my
window open.

I couldn't hear what went on inside the car and lived
with a low-grade headache—the result of the cold
mountain air blowing on my left ear—all the time. The
conversation in the car, limited until now to Mickey
and I, dried up. The only sounds were the wind whis-

tling in my window, the seepage from Eric's Discman, and Dexter's occasional barks in response to Mickey's continual low hum of chatter.

We stopped more often. None of the three boys (Dexter was definitely a boy) ever needed to pee at the same time no matter how much I pushed for synchronization. We'd pull over to let Mickey take Dexter for a piddle, then half an hour later for Mickey, then another thirty minutes and it was Eric's turn.

I tried banning drinks in the car, but it didn't help. All three of them loaded up before we pulled out and when we stopped for lunch or snacks and, like camels at an oasis, consumed enough liquid to forestall dehydration for three days. Not that we were ever on the road for longer than three or four hours. Anyway, the car quickly resumed its intended function as a traveling drinks dispenser.

We carried everything. When we stopped in crowded parking lots, I was tempted to set up shop. Eric could make a sign. Pop, all kinds, including both major brands of cola, orange, root beer, cherry, lime, club soda (for me), ginger ale, diet and regular, and cream soda; Gatorade; spring water; iced tea, sweetened or not; apple, orange and grape juice, not to mention tomato; chocolate milk; and whatever slurpees we had picked up at the last stop. We were awash in liquid.

Mickey experimented with various ways of feeding and watering Dexter. The first night we bought regular bright yellow plastic feeding dishes, but they were made for stay-at-home dogs. So we bought dishes with weighted bottoms. Better, but Dexter thought they were toys and spent feeding times skidding them along the pavement as if he were in a pub at the shuffleboard table. I hoped this wouldn't prove to be an indication of his natural proclivities. A puppy was bad enough, one who drank beer, played pool and shuffleboard, and used all his spare quarters to play old Hank Williams tunes would be too much.

The three of them spent hours playing this game, slowing our forward progress even more. Next we bought metal mixing bowls, three of them nested in a neat pile, from a small-town hardware store. Mickey gingerly held the bowls, the middle size for food, the largest for water, while Dexter ate and drank. We settled on this final method and drastically increased our laundry bill.

I started combining my nightly laundry expeditions with my phone calls to Susan. Neither of us was sleeping. Once I left the room, I couldn't go back until dawn broke. Dexter uttered a quiet woof when I opened the door in daylight, but he barked hysterically, waking the entire motel (excluding Eric, who slept the night through as if he were a vampire in his daylight coffin) if I tried to return in the dark. Luckily, the sun came up earlier each day so I was usually able to sneak home by four-thirty.

After I was sure the boys were asleep, I crept out of the room, locked it, put a padlock on the handle and went to the car for the day's laundry. I picked up the clothes, the bag containing soap and bleach, and my mother in her gray plastic tub. She kept me company.

Susan and I learned to get by on catnaps. For me, that meant a couple of hours in the early morning after a quick walk with Dexter, a couple of hours, sometimes, late in the afternoon while the boys amused themselves in the pool, if there was one and it wasn't raining, or at the video arcade, or with Dexter.

Oh, yeah, Dexter. The vet in Nelson, head of the animal shelter in addition to his paying job, said no one had reported him missing. "I see lots of this in the summer," he said. "People take their pets on trips and then abandon them. They think doing it so far from home absolves them of responsibility. By the looks of this one—" he wrinkled his nose at Dexter's general scruffiness and visible rib cage "—I'd say he's been on his own for a week or ten days. Good thing you found him."

Then he kindly called him a Lab/shepherd cross. But I thought his floppy ears came from some other species altogether, as did his red coat, and his ridiculous grin. I mostly tried to ignore the size of his paws, but when they landed smack on my belly, I couldn't help myself. I had to look at them. They were huge. My hope was that he was a slow-growing breed and wouldn't achieve his full growth for years. I prayed he didn't take after Eric, who seemed to gain twenty muscular pounds and at least two inches every week.

The dog needed little to keep him happy. Companionship. Mickey was his first choice, then Eric, then me, but I'd seen him content with a complete stranger once she or he discovered that spot behind his ear. Food, any kind and lots of it. And travel. Dexter was a traveling dog, just like we'd become traveling people.

We were used to the different rhythm of the road, its stops and starts, its odd combination of boredom and diversion. The sameness of the roads, the anticipation of the next corner or valley or town. And with Mickey's avid perusal of maps and glossy brochures and crooked hand-done pages plucked from bulletin boards or telephone poles, we had an enormous choice of attractions.

Dexter loved the car. Worshipped new smells and sounds and places. Everything excited him and his enthusiasm was contagious. Although he tried to hide it, even Eric felt it. I felt it once I got used to not sleeping.

One night, Susan said, "I feel just like I did when the boys were babies. That weird low-level anxiety that goes with getting woken up every couple of hours."

"Yeah, me too. I can't sleep longer than that anymore, and when I get the chance to sleep, I wake up. And then I start to worry."

"I used to lie in bed listening to Don snore, and the

babies breathe on the baby monitor, and pack an earthquake bag in my mind. I did it over and over again, putting things in, taking others out, until I got it exactly right. It took about three months. The very next day I went out and bought everything. I didn't even need a list, and once I bought that stuff, I stopped worrying about it. Weird, huh?"

I nodded. "Uh-huh."

"But a couple of months after that I started to get up and move the crib away from the window, take down the bookshelves and the paintings and then get up before Don and move everything back."

I laughed, but I knew exactly how she felt. I waffled about telling her. She didn't need to know how stressed I was. But that day at her bedside had transformed our relationship and I wasn't the strong one anymore.

"I bought canisters of pepper spray the day before we left," I said. "I sleep with it under my pillow and I keep another in the door in the car, and one in my purse. After the boys are asleep, I put a chair under the doorknob and bottles on all the windowsills. I have a screwdriver in my purse and I unplug all the lights and the TV, and unscrew the air conditioner."

I knew Susan was grinning, though she was kinder than me, she didn't laugh.

"I pick a motel with its own laundry or a Laundromat across the street and a room I can see from there.

I sit on the floor beside their bed and breathe with them, as if my breathing will make sure they don't stop."

This time, she laughed.

"I did that, too. I remember when Eric was little and had those terrible ear infections. I'd force myself to sleep with the same side of my head on the pillow night after night until my ear ached with the pressure. By then, the antibiotics had kicked in and he was fine. I'd wake up with a sore ear and think, *ah, I've got it instead of Eric.* But I got over all that, stopped being so anxious, learned to sleep all over again. I think it's back because they're so far away."

The anxiety was back because she had just got out of the hospital minus both breasts, and now faced weeks of chemotherapy and then more of radiation, because our mother had died of the same disease. The boys being with me was supposed to lessen her anxiety, not add to it.

"Do you want us to come home?" *Please say yes,* I thought with my fingers crossed.

"God, no. I'm glad they're gone. I'd be worried about them as well. I know I'll be able to sleep again soon. Once I get used to the silence."

I didn't know that. I couldn't remember a time when I wasn't anxious, although I couldn't have been this way in my twenties. Could I? No way I'd have gone on all those blind dates, drunk so much, driven off for the weekend at a moment's notice. No, the anxiety started some-time after that, although I couldn't pinpoint its arrival.

Like spring in Toronto, one day it was simply there. The day before I'd been fine, carrying on with my life. Oh, sometimes, if I'd been on vacation and spent more than I planned, or had been partying too hard, I worried about money. But one day I woke up and I fretted about everything. I blamed it on the tequila from the night before and vowed, yet again, to stop drinking. For one week, I didn't go out, didn't drink a single glass of wine or beer or tequila. I convinced myself I'd be fine once all the alcohol left my bloodstream. Every time I peed, I pictured the loss of anxiety.

But it didn't go away. I tried drinking, exercise, yoga, prescriptions, meditation. I must have read a hundred self-help books before I resigned myself to its presence. Nothing I did put a dent in it.

And it grew as I got older. Its grip tightened, affect-ing more and more of my life. It was the reason I hadn't gone back to visit Auntie Mabel. By the time I wanted to, having got past the loves and hates, ups and downs, ins and outs of my wild twenties—never so wild as I might have wished but often more complicated than I could cope with—the anxiety had its claws into me. I might have gone if I could get there by bus or train or car but I couldn't get on a plane. Not by myself. And neither Susan nor my mother would go with me.

It manifested itself in small ways at first, things I could work around without too much trouble. Couldn't fly? Auntie Mabel would still be there next year. Besides, I was too busy with work or a new boyfriend or whatever continuing education class I was taking that year. Flying was easy to avoid, lots of people hated to fly.

But it got worse. I started waking in the night and worrying about disasters: atomic bombs, earthquakes, tsunamis, hurricanes. My fear was indiscriminate. Lying in bed and waiting for the house to move around me, imagining a whole scenario, most of it ripped right from the screenplays of disaster movies. I survived, shaken but unhurt.

I spent days crossing the city, fighting off crazed looters, building rafts to get across inlets where bridges had collapsed, helping dig victims from the rubble, until finally, after days without sleep or food or water, on my last legs, I reached Susan's house, a pile of boards and mortar, the condemned sign already hanging from the backboard of the basketball hoop in the driveway. No one knew if they lived or died. I made my way to the hospital. They'd not been there, if I could believe the cruelly overburdened nurse at the desk. The makeshift mortuary filled with bodies. No sign of them. In my imaginings, I went on looking for them, giving up only when the sun came up and I got out of bed and into the shower.

I stopped going away on weekends. What if something happened while I was away and they couldn't find me? What if I was an accident victim and no one knew who I was? Still, these anxieties weren't serious; I could live with them. Who needed sleep? Or vacations?

But then it was bridges. A real problem. Well, it wasn't the bridges themselves, but the combination of earthquakes and bridges. What if an earthquake occurred while I was on a bridge? I'd seen the news stories of what happened in San Francisco and Los Angeles. That was where people died. Right there, by being unlucky enough to be on some bridge or overpass at that exact instant and kaboom! Your life was over. So bridges had to go. But I lived in a city filled with them.

Water lurked everywhere: creeks, rivers, lakes, inlets, even an ocean. I could get from home to work without going over a bridge by adding half an hour to my commute. I could go almost anywhere the long way around without a bridge, but I couldn't get to my mother's house. So I stopped going. And because I refused to tell her the truth, I quickly ran out of reasonable excuses. And then out of unreasonable ones.

And then we fought.

"You're ungrateful and selfish," she said. "I worked my whole life for you and your sister and now I'm old and tired and you can't find the time to visit me."

There was nothing new about this line, nothing

out of the ordinary. It didn't matter what I did or didn't do. I was the ungrateful one and Susan the perfect one.

"I'm busy, Mum. Work's tough right now. Layoffs, fluctuating interest rates, bankruptcies, foreclosures." I tried to impress her, to show her what an important job I had. I shouldn't have bothered. They were excuses, and lousy ones at that. "How about next week?"

She harrumphed and hung up. I didn't blame her. I'd been saying the same thing for months. I'd seen her only at Susan's since bridges became out of the question.

The next conversation was even worse because I had been avoiding her, screening my calls, not returning hers. By the time we spoke—she caught me at the office where I didn't expect her—I'd already lost the battle and knew it. She had me on the defensive before she even said a word. And then, to top it all off, she surprised me. Shocked might be a better word.

"Randy."

"Mum. Hi."

"What's wrong, honey? Are you sick? I know something's bothering you."

God. I could bear her usual guilt trips, her anger, her dislike of me and my job and my lifestyle, her continuous nagging about grandchildren, but I couldn't bear her concern. It was too unusual.

"I'm fine. Everything's fine."

"Are you eating properly? I could make some meals for your freezer."

"I'm eating fine, Mum."

The lie came out without a hitch. I lived by myself—of course I didn't eat right. For weeks on end, I lived on microwave popcorn and takeout food. KFC, Chinese, subs, giant bags of potato chips chased with chocolate.

"Have you had a check-up? Maybe you're a little anemic?"

"I went for a physical last month. Everything's perfect. Better than perfect. Dr. Cameron said my blood pressure was so low she thought I'd fall asleep on the examining table."

Another lie. But they were getting harder. Now I felt compelled to embellish them.

"How's work going? They'd never lay you off, would they? You're too valuable, and you've been there forever."

Those were exactly the reasons they would lay me off.

"There aren't any layoffs at my level, Mum. They don't need to, it's really just tellers and clerks. You know, automation is changing the way we service our customers."

The biggest lie yet. The office was like a school on the first day of summer holidays. The empty offices echoed around me. There used to be almost fifty of us, now we were down to ten.

"There's nothing wrong with me. I'm just busy." My voice shook to match my hands.

"It's Tom, isn't it? He's dumped you just like all the others. Why can't you be more like Susan?"

Yeah, more like my sister, raising two boys without a father, never dating, running herself ragged trying to be everything to Eric and Mickey. Just what I wanted. My already wobbling control exploded into a million raging pieces.

"I—don't—want—to—be—like—Susan." My teeth clenched so tightly I barely got the words out. "She's too much like you."

I expected the cheap plastic phone to shatter in my hands when I hung up, but it didn't. I expected a bolt of lightning to strike me right through the climate-controlled window. No such luck. Worst of all, I expected the phone to ring so she could rage back at me but it didn't.

The anxiety escalated, but it was a creeping kind of enemy, mustard gas rather than a howitzer. By the time I recognized the symptoms of what was bothering me, I'd already given up whatever was causing them. I gave up movies except for matinees. I didn't like arriving home alone after dark. I gave up hiking. Broken ankles or falling into an unseen canyon. Canoeing. Swimming. Hamburgers unless I cooked them myself.

My world was contracting in on itself. I thought of

the anxiety as a black hole, sucking my life into it, absorbing all the energy I once had for living. Now I tried to get through the day, gingerly picking my way, moving across a minefield, each step a potential disaster.

Susan said the anxiety would pass. Maybe hers would but I wasn't so confident about mine. I'd lived with it for so long I couldn't imagine a life without it.

And neither could I imagine a life any more without these peaceful nighttime hours in strange towns, sitting in the bright fluorescent light of the warm, sweet-smelling laundry rooms, alone yet somehow less lonely than I'd been for years. The soft hum of the machines lulled me into what might pass for sleep, a kind of meditative relaxation.

I put Mum on top of a dryer so she was at eye level from the orange plastic chair that seemed to have been shipped ahead of me across the prairies from town to town. I leaned back in the chair, put my feet up against the dryer. The warmth and buzz of movement simulated the motion of the car. We both liked it.

She sat there on top of the dryer quietly listening as I spoke to Susan. But it was those hours just before dawn when things started to change between us. After Susan hung up, the anxiety I'd been able to keep at bay rushed back to overpower me again. I had been talking to her ever since she moved out of the trunk of my old car onto my bookshelf, but never about anything important, only superficial conversation. Now, in laundry room after laundry room I continued the art I'd learned in Susan's hospital room.

I talked, for the first time in my life, of things I'd ignored, things so black and ugly I cringed as I spoke of them. I whispered the stories of my abortion and the shame I still felt. I told her of the night I'd been raped—date rape they would call it now. I told her about the month I'd spent praying for the blood to appear on my toilet paper and how I'd fainted, cracking my head open on the sink, when I saw it. I pulled back my hair to show her the faint scar from the stitches.

"Dennis was a disaster," I said. "I think all my problems are his fault."

I felt, rather than heard, her hiss of disapproval. One of her favorite ideas was that our problems were of our own making—my problems, that is, not hers. I spoke for her. I spoke her words.

"Yeah, can't blame Dennis. I never should have got involved with him in the first place. Why didn't you tell me before it was too late?"

But even that blatant provocation didn't open her mouth and I eventually tired of answering my own questions, playing my own therapist. I'd close my eyes and wake with a start when the dryer shut off. I'd fold the clothes, hugging their warmth to my chest, staring out the window at the door of our room, anticipating the moment the sky would change from black to gray and never quite catching it.

The change was so subtle it was impossible to chart, just as our change—me and Eric and Mickey and now Dexter—to travelers had crept up on us so slowly I couldn't say when or how it happened, only that it had. We were comfortable on the road. That was it. Each morning, we settled into the car as into a warm bath, sinking into our accustomed places, the smells of our journey familiar, sweet like a favorite bath oil.

Eric's Notebook Lunchtime

Dexter. What a stupid name for a dog. Suits him though. He's stupid too. Just like Mickey and Randy, thinking everything is okay. They smile too much.

I used to smile. Before Mum got sick, before I saw her in the hospital. Before they cut her up. When she looked okay. Is her hair falling out? She never says. Now there's nothing to smile about.

I can't draw. The only good thing I've done since Mum started dying is that dragonfly. And I copied that. Some Indian painted it hundreds of years ago and it's way better than what I do today.

I was fooling myself about being a painter. I've lost it, all my talent, that is. Old Graham told me I had extraordinary talent. Gave me an A+ in

Art. Put my painting on the cover of the yearbook and I wasn't even in Grade 12. But he wouldn't do that now. No way. He'd look at this and his face would wrinkle up like he smelled crap on my shoes or something.

The dragonfly, though, it's good. That guy really knew what he was doing. With only one color of paint. I wonder if he used his own blood? It's kind of that color. Nah. Of course not.

So maybe that's what I should do. One color. That rust Conte. Just try it. Can't be any worse than what I'm doing. I could draw Dexter if he'd stand still for one minute.

CHAPTER 7

Do not allow your specimens (once collected) to get dirty.
—*The Sunshine Coast News*, September 15, 2005

We finally popped out of the Rockies at Hinton, Alberta, one hundred kilometers east of Jasper. A new province, finally, but with at least two thousand kilometers added onto the official mileage of 965 kilometers. We were days late. We'd acquired Dexter and all his accoutrements, the car seemed more like home than home, and Eric had smiled. Once. I gave up sleeping, Mickey gave up the front seat, and Eric gave up silence, replacing it with a few well-chosen words directed mostly at Dexter.

Dexter adored Mickey, but he listened to Eric.

"Sit," and Dexter's butt hit the ground with an audible thud.

"Down," and Dexter took his wet grubby paws off yet another stranger's legs.

The relationship between the three of them looked and sounded like a family in a black-and-white television show. I couldn't help but picture Mickey in an apron, saying to Dexter, "Just wait until your father gets home," and Eric in a suit and skinny tie opening the door at exactly five-thirty and calling out, "Honey, I'm home," and then solving all the problems between the kids and their mother, a perfect combination of Solomon and Marcus Welby, M.D. The odd thing to me was how naturally they filled their roles. Even Dexter played his part with perfect aplomb.

We had left Nelson heading north for Banff and Lake Louise, but none of us liked the crowds. Especially Dexter. Well, he loved the crowds but was uncontrollable. Japanese tourists screamed at the sight of him galumphing up to them, and the volume increased when they felt the weight of his paws on their clothes. Even as a puppy, Dexter was plenty big enough to scare them, though Mickey pointed out they were happy enough to walk up to a two-ton elk or even a bear to get a photograph.

So he suggested we hang a sign around Dexter's neck. Wild Siberian Husky. The tourists wouldn't know the difference and Dexter's picture would soon grace photograph albums all over the world. We spent most of the day creating new species. Mickey tended toward the fantastic: Blue Mountain Dragon Dog, High Plains

Griffin, Transylvanian Vampire Dog. Eric's names were skewed to rock and roll: Korn Wolf and Limp Bizkit Bi-Dog. Mine were too boring to mention. We settled, in the end, on Mickey's favorite and Dexter was officially christened a Blue Mountain Dragon Dog. Eric made a sign, with a picture background. We attached it to his harness and waited for the next opportunity to use it.

It soon arrived on the Icefields Parkway from Banff to Jasper. We were crammed in between tour bus after tour bus laden with tourists. The buses, and the people in them, were like a school of fish or a herd of migrating caribou, moving in perfect synchronization—speed, distance, turns, all choreographed in some divine harmony.

We drove the whole way breathing diesel fumes and seeing the sights out the side windows. The front and back views were close-ups of huge silver expanses embossed with names like Embassy Tours, Great Pacific Sightseeing, and Exquisite Panoramic Sights Guaranteed. No way to get around them, either. I passed half a dozen buses before I realized that the entire route was packed, mile after smelly mile, with buses occasionally interspersed with an almost-as-large RV or a rare car looking cowed, as if any moment it might be crushed between a pair of hurtling behemoths.

I settled back, my eyes on the license plate in front of me, and concentrated on matching my speed to the pack. It was mindless driving, which suited me fine.

That was how I felt. Each day, more distanced from the woman I'd been only a month before. That woman had a job, a carefully controlled and calm life, without anything to disturb her. A job I did without thought, the few skills it required long part of my subconscious. No permanent man. No kids. Perfect freedom. Perfect emptiness. A woman without a care in the world. At least that's how I played it.

Now, though, the miles of driving and the sleepless nights were accomplishing something I wasn't too happy about. That woman, the one I was used to and comfortable with, was receding, quickly, like high tide rushing out from a long, flat beach, leaving me stranded and alone and scared shitless, like a starfish drowning in the air. I felt myself losing the bright protective coloring I'd painstakingly created over the years and turning a kind of pallid gray.

I had bought books in Nelson, four days ago, and hadn't cracked the covers. A box of magazines, articles and classic novels I always meant to read nestled next to my mother in the trunk. I hadn't opened the box, my hands passing over it as if it weren't there.

The low hum of the tires on the highway, the wind whistling through the window, the distant tinny voices of Eric's music, Mickey in the back seat speaking softly in Dexter's ear, these faint repetitive sounds worked on me like a mantra. I felt myself falling further into mindlessness with each passing mile, and I no longer, thanks to the lack of sleep, had the energy to fight it.

Mickey made all the route decisions, plus began the round of stops. He blamed it on Dexter, but he knew me well enough to know what would work. Even I couldn't expect a three-month-old puppy to wait *just another half hour, okay?* Although that ploy sometimes worked with Mickey and Eric.

I fought the first stop, wanting to keep moving, my foot on the gas pedal, my body encased in its familiar seat. I didn't know what might happen when we stopped. We'd phone Susan, Mickey would get lost again, another tourist would be traumatized by Dexter or he'd race off down the hill and end up in the river. And we'd have to find sticks and ropes and climbing equipment, belay down the hill and fish him out, somehow. This would occasion dry clothes for all of us and a half-hour wait while we dried Dexter. Something always happened when we stopped.

Driving made me feel safe. I didn't have to make any decisions. The road from Banff to Jasper, surrounded by buses determining my speed, was the best so far. We stopped when the bus in front did, ate with eighty Japanese tourists. Their voices, in a language I couldn't understand, allowed me to stay in what I called the zone—that place where I thought about nothing, worried about nothing, simply followed directions (from

Mickey or the driver of the bus in front of me or the signs on the highway warning me to slow to seventy), and placed one foot in front of the other. Easy-peasy. No stress, no worry, no anxiety.

I loved those few hours each day when we were on the road in our cocoon. Mickey, Eric and Dexter hated them. So each day turned into a tug-of-war, me at one end of the rope trying to stay in the car and keep moving, and the three of them on the other, counseling stop after stop. The three of them, of course, won the tug-of-war, and I felt myself fading further.

We'd been on the road for over a week, a routine well established. It was working for the boys. They seemed to become more confident, more comfortable, more secure in themselves the longer we traveled. Their conversations with Susan—what I heard of them—sounded more like boys' chatter. The long silences, the uncomfortable pauses, the ums and ahs, became fewer every day. Dexter was mostly responsible for that. There was always a puppy story to tell. Besides, even I could hear the strength and cheerfulness returning to Susan's voice. But they were still fighting. I had no energy to deal with it and I no longer mentioned it to Susan.

The two of them had entered into a conspiracy. Neither of them spoke to Susan of anything difficult. Sometimes I wished it were true they had no problems, but then I saw Eric's face or heard the catch in Mickey's voice and longed for the skill and the courage to draw them out. But I had neither and so we continued to travel, each of us locked in our own heads, coming out only in the most practical of ways. Food, drink, motels, rest stops, tourist attractions, laundry and telephone. These were our topics of conversation. And Dexter, of course.

The dark of night, the quiet humming of the dryer, my mother in her gray plastic tub, the sweet smell of clean laundry, were the things that returned my voice to me. Each night, in those few hours between midnight and dawn, I spoke of more than where we would find our next meal or make our next stop. I voiced my fear, my anxiety, my desire to lose myself in the journey.

Oh, not to Susan. I was a silent partner in the boys' conspiracy. We spoke of anxiety, but only in the past tense. Of fear, but never in the present, never for the future. We talked of old boyfriends, ruinous relationships, but never of anything new, never of a man for me. We laughed about the boys and Dexter. I played my city girl role to the max.

No, I spoke the truth only to my mother. I didn't think too clearly about it, but if I had, I would have realized two things were jumbled up in my mind. Speaking to her was safe. She wouldn't say anything to contradict me or give me advice, and I'd never see her raise her eyebrows or twist her mouth again. And way back in the depths of my mind, in counterpoint, was the fantasy. If I talked long enough, she would reply.

And her response would be loving and positive.

I'm proud of you, she'd say. *You're my favorite daughter.*

And I'd grin and shuffle my feet and say, *Aw shucks*, but I'd be waiting for her to say more of the things I'd waited a lifetime to hear.

You're strong and brave and beautiful, Miranda Jane.

I smiled at that. *Not beautiful, Mum.*

Your father thought you more beautiful than the morning sun or the evening star, more beautiful than life itself.

My imagination faltered at that. My mother might, two years after her death, be willing to praise me—it cost her nothing—but there was no way, no matter how many years passed, that she would tell me those things about my father. Auntie Mabel had put those words into my head, and it was her voice I heard, not my mother's. Never, not those words. So I sat back in my orange plastic chair, put my feet up on the dryer, and started talking.

"You loved him, didn't you? He was your life. Never me. I took him away from you."

The tub on the dryer shivered slightly, as if in response.

"But why Susan? That's what I don't get. Why did you love her and not me?"

It was a question I'd lived with as long as I could re-

member. It colored my whole life. My relationships—
with her and with Susan, of course, but with everyone
else as well. That insecurity was the bedrock of my personality. That my mother loved my sister, not simply
better than me, but at all. Because, in my mind, she had
only ever loved my father.

"What changed in that year?"

I barely heard my voice over the thumping of
Mickey's runners cascading around in the dryer. It
didn't matter, I knew she heard me. Another tiny
shiver, a slight movement on the chipped white
enamel. Oh, yeah, she heard me all right.

"He was lost already. That's it, isn't it? He loved me
and you thought that meant he didn't love you anymore. You were wrong, you know. Way wrong."

Eric and Mickey and Susan had taught me that.
Until Susan had children, I thought like my mother.
Only one love at a time. If I loved a man, I couldn't love
Susan or my mother, no room for them. Not at the
same time. Loving meant an all-out, full-speed-ahead
kind of passion.

I learned that from my mother, and it took almost
thirty years for me to unlearn it. She never did. My
mother loved my father, so she had no space to love me.
When I was born and my father loved me, she waited
for Susan to be born and then she loved her. Still no
room for me. One love, that was it.

But when Eric was born, I loved him from the very first time I saw him, and watching Susan's face as she fed him, I learned I could still love her at the same time. When Mickey, five weeks premature, lay in his plastic world fighting for life, I loved him, and loved Susan and Eric more because of it.

Dr. Seuss was right. My heart burst its bounds and grew right there on the spot. Even at the time, standing in the dim light of the neonatal intensive-care ward, I knew how corny it was to be comparing myself to the Grinch, but I couldn't help it.

The Grinch was my hero. Every year I started checking the television listings in October so I wouldn't miss him. There was something about the Grinch that drew me, sucked me right in, even as a hostile teenager, even as a sophisticated grown up. It was the first video I bought even though I never watched it that way. I was used to the rhythm of the television show, waiting through the commercials, slowing it down, making the climax more exciting.

My conversation with my mother wasn't over, probably wouldn't ever be, but I was too tired to go on. I knew I wouldn't sleep but I closed my eyes, hoping for a moment's respite. My days were split in half as if someone had ripped apart a piece of paper. One side, the daylight part, was mindless, slow, without tension. The other half, the night side, was filled with revelations, anger, passion. But I couldn't put the two together, I didn't have the right glue, or steady enough hands. The edges wouldn't meet.

So I felt like half a person—the physical half living in the light, the emotional me living in the dark. I had no idea what would happen if I could put them together, and I didn't want to know. The segregation kept me safe.

CHAPTER 8

> Vegetation is highly worthy of our attention; and
> in itself is of the utmost consequence to man-
> kind, and productive of many of the greatest com-
> forts and elegancies of life.
> —Gilbert White, *Natural History & Antiquities of
> Selborne*

The sun flooded the day with lemon-scented light. He shouted for joy, his voice bouncing off the boxes piled high around him, echoing through the many empty rooms. The sound set in play the layers of dust, forcing them into the air for a brief moment before they settled again, like old men on a stoop, standing to stretch their aching legs then relaxing back into their chairs. The dust belonged. He wasn't sure if he did. But it didn't matter. He was here.

"I'm free. Lord God above, I'm finally free."

Tom Webb's face ached from the unaccustomed exercise, stretching, smiling from the minute he woke, rising from his makeshift bed to greet the sun until, finally, long after the late northern sunset, he headed for the porch and his sleeping bag.

The house needed far more work than he had realized at first sight last October. He was driving through Cranberry Portage on the final leg of a fall collecting trip, racing to get home before the first snowfall. He had arrived in town after dark, but he was overtired and couldn't relax into his ratty motel room.

Too many uncomfortable beds, too many moldy showers behind him. Too many nights watching a snowy television screen flickering CBC North, too long eating greasy takeout. Too many packages of specimens sent back to the office and still his trunk was full. Enough. He was tired. He wanted to go home. So he walked the deserted streets, examining trees and shrubs, their naked bones shining through the few leaves clinging to the branches.

Cranberry Portage. It was his first visit, the first visit in many years by anyone connected with his department. That wasn't unusual. Many of the shrinking towns in the north got short shrift from the government and, from what Tom gathered, the townspeople didn't much care. Self-sufficient and self-reliant, they preferred to carry on without interference from the south.

The only light accompanying him on his walk filtered out through the curtains in living rooms and kitchens along his path.

"Dork," he muttered as he tripped over another rock. "No sidewalks and no streetlights. Pretty, though." Tom had spent six weeks this trip in various northern towns and had, over the years, probably visited hundreds of them. This one seemed different. To entertain himself, he tried to figure out why. Maybe because after this he was going home? But it looked different.

Many of the houses in this neighborhood, even in the dark, were easily identified as army issue. He walked through, he guessed, what were once the married officer's quarters. Short, boxlike houses, he imagined them in their heyday, each identical, looking, in their conformity and spruceness, like a row of their own occupants on parade. Now, though, some of them sported paint jobs the army would have court-martialed for—turquoise and yellow, even lavender and shell-pink—the colors visible in the ring of light around each door, a courtesy northern inhabitants extended to their visitors to compensate for the long winter afternoons.

It didn't help Tom much, though, as he tripped over yet another rock, this time falling to his knees on the gravel at the side of the road. He headed for the lights ahead, presumably the town center.

The Mid Northern Line was the cause of the boom and its withdrawal the cause of the crash. He'd been in other towns that hadn't weathered the move as well. Cranberry Portage looked to have spunk. As he walked through downtown, he examined the storefronts—hardware and bakery and clothing, a shoe store, a hairdresser and two coffee shops—every one of them gleaming in the streetlights. The town councillors must have decided to light this central block, although, like most towns this far north, once Labor Day was over, everything closed up in late afternoon so the inhabitants could get home and cuddle into their warm, cozy houses and ignore the creeping darkness outside.

Tom passed through the commercial district and headed down a small hill. This part of Cranberry Portage harbored a wholly different breed of houses. The big old Victorian at the end of Main Street caught his eye. It stood at the corner, windows blind, uncurtained in the night. This house could use some of the color and light displayed in the other half of town. A few of the windows were broken, haphazardly boarded up. The shutters hung askew, the chimneys had shed some of their bricks. Its paint hung from the siding in strips, giving it the look of a room being stripped of generations of wallpaper, but there was something about it, a hidden life buried beneath the raggedness, beckoning to Tom. Under this unfortunate exterior, it seemed to say, is a house for a lifetime. I'm still sound under here, still beautiful. You have eyes to see this.

A ragged For Sale sign hung from its porch, the phone number almost indecipherable in the gloom.

Tom pulled a flashlight from his pocket and traced the name and number with his fingertips, deciphering the code, compelled by an undeniable urge. He laughed out loud at that thought and believed, for a moment, that the house laughed with him. Tom Webb was not a man who had undeniable urges, except for peanut M&M's. He prided himself on being a scientist, a practical, logical, left-brain kind of guy. But this house...

There was a charm hidden under the layers of neglect and, standing there in the cold night, Tom Webb, for the first time in his life, succumbed. With his government-issue Bic pen he wrote the name and phone number of the Realtor on the lined notepad he kept in his jacket pocket. He stood on the rickety porch and rearranged not just his schedule for the next week to include a visit to the Realtor, but his entire life. By the time he stepped back into the street, unaware of being chilled to the bone, his simple, straightforward life was changed beyond all recognition.

The next day he phoned the Realtor in a slightly bigger town two hundred kilometers south and by noon, without a second thought or look at the house, he signed an offer and wrote a check. Within a week Tom Webb, safe, secure civil servant on the upward ladder, gave six months' notice and started liquidating his assets and making lists.

That moment on the porch had changed his life, a

life he hadn't even known needed changing. But once he'd done it, he felt as if some giant had stooped down out of the clouds and removed a Canadian Shield rock from his shoulders, as if another giant had transformed the muscles in his face so his natural expression was a grin instead of the frown he wore in every single picture in his photograph album and those of his parents before him.

Lighter, he spent the cold Winnipeg winter whistling as he warmed his car in the morning, humming as he raced through the office, laughing out loud at the expressions on the faces of his fellow employees, an awkward combination of envy, despair and glee at his foolishness. No one understood the impulse driving him, and no one, including Tom, cared to. He was too busy planning.

He got a friend, a surveyor, to go over the property, and to draw him a plan of the house he now owned and hadn't seen the inside of. So he had the dimensions of the rooms—all eleven of them, plus a basement, garage and assorted outbuildings. He ignored the friend, who tried to tell him about the state of disrepair of the house, preferring to concentrate on his lists and plans and his vision of the house—his house, his first love.

And once he'd done that, drawn pictures, spent days in paint and hardware stores, bought hundreds of decorating magazines, taken half-a-dozen handyman courses—Tom was a pretty good journeyman carpenter from his years in the bush, building makeshift shelters—but he had no idea about plumbing or electricity or, God forbid, decorating.

The decor of his house in Elmwood consisted of walls full of mismatched bookshelves. The closest thing to home decorating was the long central hallway. He filled it with dozens of photographs. Lakes and rivers, sunrises and sunsets, trees and flowers. Most of them he'd taken on his collecting trips or his summer holidays, canoeing along the western rivers, northern creeks and lakes. Maybe the determining factor in his decision to buy the house had been its location, right in the heart of the Grass River system, a long leisurely world of connected lakes and creeks and rivers, celebrated for its beauty.

Tom had in the back of his mind two ways to make a living, not a lot of money, as the house was paid for, but enough to buy groceries and books and pay the taxes. He could run a bed and breakfast in the summer—that was his first idea—though when he thought of all that cooking and cleaning and socializing it made his eyes cross. Or he could, with a bit of luck, do guided canoe trips.

Over the past few years he had noticed a proliferation of European and American tourists on the lakes. But they saw only the easily accessible stuff—a couple of hours, a day at the most. Drive the car in to the lake, rent a canoe, spend a while on the water, all within sight of the marina where they'd rented the boat.

They had no way of knowing about the hidden delights, many of them soon to be right at Tom's doorstop. Three- or four-day trips into the bush, camping, cooking over a fire, spending the days gliding through the speckled light of the creeks and rivers, led by someone who knew not only canoeing, but the flora and fauna, an expert like Tom. What self-respecting tourist could ask for more?

He could put together packages for bigger groups and longer trips. This idea sprang full-blown to his mind, as if it had always been there, germinating in the cold darkness of winter, waiting only for the warmth of spring to burst into riotous bloom.

That winter he felt the oddest thing was this: unlike most of his friends and colleagues, unlike almost everyone he knew, Tom had, even through the years of midlife, continued to enjoy his life and his work, to feel fulfilled by it. He was the only one not searching, not getting divorced or having an affair, not buying a sports car or getting religion or turning into a health nut. Yet he was the one changing his life. Maybe that was why everyone around him looked at him as if he were stark raving mad.

His parents, safely retired in the eternal summer of

southern Florida, practically fell out of their matching golf shorts when he told them what he'd done.

"North? You're moving up north?" His dad, born and bred in the northern tundra, had become a born-again believer in unlimited sunshine and he spread the gospel at every opportunity.

"If you want out of the city, come down here." He spread his arms to embrace his world of condos and malls, all basking under the harsh December sun.

Tom shivered at the thought of it. Bathing suits in December? Sure, the women looked great strolling by in their bikinis, their tanned bodies glowing. But it was unnatural, all that flesh, and no snow. It was Christmas, for God's sake, and not a pine tree or snowflake in sight. Give him the real winter of the prairies.

"Lots of work in Florida," his dad continued. "Construction everywhere. They're building as if there's no tomorrow." He puffed out his chest. "This condo is worth fifteen thousand dollars more—U.S. dollars I mean—than it was last week. Thanks to that."

Tom couldn't miss it. A mall sprawled across four or five city blocks, huge neon signs beckoning to the silver swarm of cars and RVs rushing by. He nodded and smiled at his father, neither agreeing nor disagreeing.

"I love you, old man, but this is your world, not mine. I'd pine, like Monty Python's parrot, if I left the north."

"But, dear, aren't there, I mean I've heard, well, you know."

Tom and his father were used to this mode of conversation and started to coax it from her, Tom far more patiently than his father.

"No, Ma. I don't know. What do you mean?"

"Yeah, Phyllis, spit it out. Say what you mean, woman."

She blushed a shade of pink both men still, after decades in her presence, found charming. Phyllis, her energetic curls and bright eyes irresistible, smiled at her men.

"Tom. Wife. Children."

They shrugged and dug a little further.

"Okay, it's the grandchildren thing again."

Tom, in the latter half of his forties, and an only child, had spent twenty-five years fending off his mother's efforts to get him married. She'd been silent on the subject since moving to Florida but obviously hadn't given it up.

"It's just as easy to find a woman in Cranberry Portage as it is in Winnipeg."

"My point exactly." His mother's voice rang with justification.

"Huh?"

"You're forty-eight years old and I have no grandchildren. Thirty years in Winnipeg and you're still single."

"Got it."

"And…"

He waited for the coup de grâce.

"There are twice as many men as women in the north."

Tears welled in her eyes, which both men ignored. She turned them on and off at will.

"I'm never going to have grandchildren."

Tom had consoled her as best he could, but the topic stayed on the front burner during his stay. Just when he thought she'd forgotten it, it would flare up again. It was a bad time of year to visit. Everyone in the gated complex had their grandchildren visiting for the holidays, so each time he and Phyllis took a walk along the man-made canal, another old woman stopped to introduce her grandbabies.

He was glad to return to the real world of winter, glad even to spend four hours on the ground in Chicago waiting for a storm to blow over. Anything to get away from the heat and the harping.

Tom Webb had always, under the facade of government scientist and civil servant, thought of himself as a solitary man, an outdoorsman. He believed he was fulfilling his previously unacknowledged destiny by moving to Cranberry Portage, answering a call unheeded for years.

But the house might kill him before he finished. He'd arrived in town on the cusp of spring, ready to enjoy the long days, planning to spend the mornings cleaning and painting, restoring the house to glory, and the afternoons exploring the land around him. One day was all it took to disillusion him of that plan. Working all out, through the long hours of sunlight, he might make the house habitable by mid-summer. And *might* was the operative word.

It was in terrible shape. When he stepped inside the front door for the first time—having, and the regret welled in him now, chosen not to come up to Cranberry Portage until he was ready to move—he stood in the hallway, his hands chill in the damp years-old miasma. The broken windows hadn't helped with the circulation. It was as if the whole house had been buried in thick black dirt, without even earthworms to aerate it. He tried to breathe, but it hurt his chest. The house released stale air.

It reminded him of how he had once imagined the Tomb of the Pharaohs to have smelled—a musty, rank smell. Ancient lifeless air. Inhuman. He panicked and thought: *This is what happens when you intrude into dead space.* He had read about Carter and Carnarvon as a child and kept Carnarvon's picture pinned up in his lab to remind him of the dangers of ill-planned, hasty openings of long-closed doors. Carnarvon's slow painful death from inhaling cryptococcus neuromyces, the living fungus feeding on the soft tissues of his body, pouring poison into his blood. Driving him mad in the end.

But there wouldn't be any fungus in this air. The house was wood, not stone, and it hadn't been sealed up for three or four thousand years. He stopped cringing and stepped back outside. He couldn't think in the house.

He took a deep breath of the crisp spring air. While the oxygen reinvigorated his brain, he examined the parts of the house he could see. The remaining windows looked sound, the filthy glass old enough to be wavy. He stomped around the porch and up and down the steps. Firm, no soft spots.

He took three deep breaths in a row as if he were going to dive into a lake to retrieve a lost pair of glasses and reentered the house. This time the shock was less. He raced through the rooms on the main floor, jostling open the windows to let the world back in.

Once he had a cross-draft going, things improved, and he grabbed a chisel to pry open the rest of the painted-shut windows. Most of them looked as if they hadn't been cracked in years, paint grafted on in layers, built up inches thick. But once they were open, once he'd pried the plywood from the broken ones, the house brightened, shaking off some of the gloom that encompassed it. He almost caught the house smiling and nodding thanks.

The upstairs, filled with tiny airless rooms, proved no better than the main floor. The house sat on a rise, surrounded at the bottom by a fence, and although rocks might have occasionally punctured a ground-floor window, Tom doubted even he could hit a second-story one. He spent the first morning measuring the broken glass on the main floor and attending, in the first of almost daily expeditions, the hardware store down the street.

Tom had made the decision, during the optimistic planning stage in Winnipeg, to buy everything he needed, to hire contractors to do the few things he couldn't do himself, in Cranberry Portage. Not just for the goodwill or the help in his fledgling business, but for the knowledge. Lloyd Farren in the hardware store knew exactly where Tom should go for the glass and as an added bonus regaled him with a condensed history of the house, ending with a tale that must have been repeated a dozen times over.

"They were the nicest family," he said, "the Romans. He worked on the Line, a scientist I think, and she looked after the house, her house it was, her father left it to her when he died—the McLean house, belonged in the family, oh, since it was built."

Tom smiled. His connection to the house was explained. Of course Mr. Roman had been a scientist. He knew the house had stayed in the MacLean family since it was built, searched the public records for information about his predecessors. The house had passed in an almost unbroken line for seventy-five years, since the day Donald MacLean helped settle Cranberry Portage and bought the land.

"The girls were as cute as buttons, always together, and dressed alike, too. But you'd never mistake one for the other. The older girl, now what was her name? An unusual one." He shook his head. "Doesn't matter, I guess, but she was a ball of fire, more energy than a summer storm. And smart, sassy, too. The little one, Susan was her name, followed her sister around like a lost puppy."

Tom, to encourage Lloyd, said, "You've had the store since then?" Although Lloyd obviously didn't need any encouragement, he was in his glory talking to a new listener.

"Yep, and my father before me. Ben Roman was a good man. Loved to canoe, like you, spent almost every one of his days off out in the bush somewhere. Took the wife and girls with him most times. But the last trip…"

"What happened?" By now, Tom was as fascinated by the story as the storekeeper.

"It was late in the season, October I guess, and the girls were at school. So Ben went off on his own, just for a few hours, he said, last trip of the season. Never came back. After dark, Mrs. Roman called the RCMP and they started searching for him early the next morning. Wasn't till two days later they found the canoe floating upside down in Paint Lake, another two days before the divers found him. They figured he must have driven to Thompson and then went over to Paint Lake.

"That was the end of that family. Mrs. Roman sold off the house and before the winter set in they were gone. I think they moved out to the Coast. Might see them this summer, though."

He handed Tom a hand-printed sheet of blue paper. "It's the first ever Cranberry Portage Reunion. Maude told me she'd found the Romans. I'd like to see how those girls grew up. They were a spark of color around here."

Eric's Notebook Saturday

We made it out of the mountains. Back to the real world, lights, camera, action. But I don't like it any more than before. The only place I want to be is home.

I know I should try and be more cheerful. Mum told me that last night. Smile, Eric, she said, it's not as bad as you think.

But it is. It's worse. Everyone's pretending. Mickey's pretending to be a happy little boy. Randy's pretending to like being with us. Mum's pretending she's okay. Me and Dexter are the only ones who aren't lying.

I'm worried. About all of us. Yeah, specially about Mum, but Mickey too. He reminds me of a wind-up toy. Wind him up in the morning and he chatters all day. Smiles all day, even when no one is watching.

But at night he's different. I can feel him crying himself to sleep. He makes the bed shake. Just a little, but I feel it. I wish I could tell him everything was going to be okay, but I know it isn't. Nothing will ever be the same.

Randy's trying hard. I can see her trembling all the time, though. Her hands, and her eyes. Her lips, mostly. She's a mess.

We're such a mess it scares me. That's why I fight with Mickey and why I don't talk. I'm scared. One night I'll phone home and there'll be no answer. And then I'll have to phone the hospital and they'll tell me she's dead.

And we won't ever be able to go home.

CHAPTER 9

Adult dragonflies have few predators but they remain subject to the laws of nature. Large spiders spin webs strong enough to catch them; sundew plants and other dragonflies eat them; in some countries, people cook them in soup or eat them as a crunchy snack.

—*The Sunshine Coast News*, September 14, 2005

We couldn't get out of Hinton fast enough. After a week spent in small towns clasped lovingly by mountains, whatever charms Hinton might have had were lost on us. The only thing the boys appreciated was the proliferation of fast-food outlets, and Dexter agreed.

He looked both astonished and delighted with his first Quarter Pounder. His ridiculous grin widened until he looked more like the Cheshire Cat than a dog. His tail threatened to raise welts on every leg within reach, and his entire body vibrated with the frenzy of joy he experienced. I sighed, knowing he'd soon learn to connect the Golden Arches with this special treat, and that we'd stop there even more often than we did now.

I appreciated Pinky's Launderette, its purple and pink bubbles facing the motel where I'd stashed the boys and Dexter once the overload of grease and hydrocarbons and sugars slowed them down a bit. Everyone talked about sugar highs, but I believed that an equal and opposite load of greasy carbohydrates—one large side of fries equaling one large pop—counteracted the sugar buzz. So the only food rule I enforced was the rule of balance. One pop or chocolate bar equaled a bag of chips or an order of fries. Never one without the other. My combination theory of fast food—one I was tempted to forward to Health Canada to help the parents of teenagers—kept the energy level at a barely contained and almost acceptable level.

Pinky's Launderette sparkled. The huge bubbles painted on its concrete exterior were matched by smaller and brighter ones on every surface inside. The effect was overwhelming, especially after a day spent in the soothing deep green of the Rockies.

The room was long and narrow, made even more so by the rows of washers and dryers ranked along both walls. Pink washers and dryers. The floor, the ceiling, the walls above the appliances, were painted a pale pink, not quite matching the enamel on the washers and dryers, which didn't quite match either the floor or the ceiling. And on every single pink surface—except the machines—floated a riot of bubbles. Large ones, small ones, little teeny tiny ones, in a rainbow of pastels. Blue, yellow, green, purple, a completely obnoxious shade of orange.

I squinted, closing each eye until the sight became bearable, just. I put the gray plastic tub on the dryer nearest to the pay phone, the phone's red-and-blue design glaringly out of place in this bright, bubbled world.

Even the picture windows across the front of the space were painted with artistically arranged opaque pastel bubbles. But I could still see the red doorway numbered 108 at the motel across the parking lot. No lights were on behind the tightly drawn curtains, no hulking shadows crept near it, no eighteen-wheeler blocked my view.

I threw the laundry into the washing machine by holding the bag over the hole in the top and letting the contents fall in while I held my breath, quickly shutting the lid. A faint scent of dog food filled the air but was soon replaced by the clean smells of Tide and Bounce.

I was alone in Pinky's. I opened the door and stood on the sidewalk, the bubbled windows glowing behind me. A soft warm wind blew across the parking lot, lifting my hair from my neck. If it weren't for the roar of trucks on the highway, the asphalt-scented heat still rising from the concrete around me, I might have been on a tropical island. When I stepped away from the door, the night sky appeared as if someone had taken a paintbrush dipped in black paint and run it quickly over a lightbulb. The stars were the sky, the blackness only barely covering them.

It was time to call Susan but, for the first time since leaving Vancouver, I wanted to put it off. I didn't want to talk to her, to anyone really. What I wanted, more than anything, was to disappear into the night, away from everyone and everything. I wanted silence, complete, deep, dark stillness like I had experienced in the tunnel.

How things had changed in a week. No longer frightened by the stillness, I craved it. An absence rather than a presence. The thought was so tempting I had to sit down on the curb and wrap my arms around my legs to stop them from walking across the parking lot and disappearing into the prairie beyond.

The stars sparkled in the night sky, Room 108 stayed safe across the way, and Pinky's bubbles colored the sidewalk. I sat on the curb, rocking myself, trying desperately to ignore the blood surging through my veins, every molecule singing *Flee, run for your life,* as if a vampire or a werewolf lurked behind me, some danger so dark and powerful no quarter could be sought, no victory possible.

I was supposed to be phoning my sister, nothing serious. I had no premonition about her. She got better every day, the spirit returning to her voice, each treatment successful. This wasn't about her; it was about me.

The huge expanse of prairie sky, unlimited by horizons, made me feel exposed. I felt myself returning to the books and movies I'd devoured as a child. I had an image of myself pegged out on a vast desert floor, my limbs straining against the rope encircling them, while a ruthless sun beat down on me. I saw myself trapped in an alley in the black of night, waiting for the werewolf who'd been stalking me, my only weapons my good heart and a table knife. Perhaps I was the target of a serial killer, a man who first seduced, then strangled his victims. I waited in my silent apartment for his arrival.

These images struck a chord with me, the sense of inchoate fear and knowing there was nothing to be done but to stand and face it. No one would be racing on a white horse across the desert to rescue me; no shy policeman would spot me in my alley or arrive, just in time, at the door of my apartment. I was on my own.

But I wasn't ready, not yet. The fears that chased me were more powerful than these stock images, more subtle and dominating than any memory of a book or movie.

I simply could not move. I knew if I took my arms from around my legs, if I stood up, I would run into the blackness and never return. So I sat rocking on the curb until my butt was numb and the warm breeze turned cool and the waves of fear and the overwhelming desire to flee receded, not completely, just enough so I could unravel myself and turn back into Pinky's Launderette instead of away, so I could pick up the phone and dial the series of numbers that connected me with my sister.

The chair was the same make and model, the same plastic, as in every other Laundromat, but it was painted pale pink and embossed with bubbles. I closed my eyes and waited for Susan to pick up the phone.

"Hi," she said, her voice sultry and ready to sink into sleep.

I crossed my fingers, hoping she wouldn't catch the fear in mine.

"Hi. How's it going over there?" It sounded fine to me, and the effort of saying it pushed the fear a little further back.

Susan giggled. "Everything's fine. Great. Perfect. Wonderful."

I hadn't heard Susan that excited since the day she bought her garage and we watched them put the sign up. Susan's Garage, it had read, All Makes, All Models. She giggled at the sign, at the sight of her ad for the Yellow Pages, at the full-page announcement in the neighborhood paper.

"Are you back at work?" It was the only thing I could think of that would make her so giddy.

"Next week, I think. Steve says I can go back then, just not to get overtired."

"Steve?"

It was so obvious I couldn't believe I'd missed it before.

"Oh, my God," I said, "you're sleeping together, aren't you?"

She giggled again. No wonder she didn't hear the tension in my voice.

"Not sleeping much, and doing everything else very carefully, but yes. He's so wonderful. I can hardly wait for you guys to get back and meet him outside of the hospital. You'll love him."

"Of course we will."

Susan had been on three dates since Don left eight years ago, every single one a mistake. She'd given up after the third one heard about Eric and Mickey and suggested she ship them out to Newfoundland to live with Don. We'd talked about it over dozens of nights since then, sitting in her living room or on the porch after the boys were in bed, a bottle of wine on the table between us.

I'd say, "At least you have the boys," and she'd smile and nod and listen while I regaled her with my most recent dating disaster. I knew she was lonely, but I couldn't believe she was as lonely as me. She had the boys and the shop. She was busy, bustling around all day and every evening, smiling and cheerful. Loneliness and Susan didn't go together in my mind, and she never tried to convince me otherwise. But hearing the joy in her voice now, I realized that I'd mistaken her patience and stamina for happiness.

Each time I had raved about another man who'd done me wrong, she'd smiled.

"It's for the best, you know," she'd say. "He wasn't good enough for my big sister."

We talked for a while about Steve and his virtues—numerous—and his past life—exciting—and his delight in her and his joy about the boys. I told her about Dexter, his attachment to Eric and Mickey, and his suddenly acquired taste for McDonald's. She laughed but I heard the energy seeping from her voice.

"The laundry's done. I'll talk to you tomorrow night."

I didn't need to see her to see the slow smile spread over her face when she said, "Hmm, sleep well, Randy."

I envied her Steve, who'd returned to her the ability to sleep and I reminded myself to call her earlier the next night. I still had this one to get through though and the sky outside the windows was as black as ever. The clock over the cash machines said three o'clock, the worst hour of the night. I wondered, fleetingly, if, like Susan, a new love might abate my insomnia, knowing all the time that it was too deeply rooted for sex to solve.

I didn't speak to the woman in the gray plastic tub. The anger against her I'd discovered over the past few nights made it impossible for me to say anything nice and, although she hadn't held with it for her own use, she had drilled it into Susan and me. *If you can't say something nice, don't say anything at all.* So I said nothing, moving carefully around her and ignoring the slight movements which I took as incitements to speech.

Randy, don't ignore me. You know I hate it when you do that. Look at me when I'm speaking to you.

I huddled deeper into the chair and put my hands over my ears.

Nice try. You think your ears are what's hearing my voice? Wake up and smell the bubbles. You can't shut me out.

I hummed.

Randy, Randy, Randy. That won't work either.

I stood up and headed for the door.

Nope, not even if you leave me here and get back in the car and drive to Jasper. I'm in your head. You're stuck with me.

"Okay, get it over with." I sat back down in the bubble chair.

I've been thinking about what you said the other night. I did love you, but you were your daddy's girl. The two of you were so close—maybe closer than I'd ever been to him—I think I was jealous. I didn't get it, not then, not ever. You were the child he wanted. I didn't understand.

Whatever I'd expected her to say it wasn't that. I

waited for the rest of it, the part that said I had stolen him from her and it was all my fault, but the voice was gone.

"Mum?" I stood up and jiggled the gray plastic tub. "You in there?"

Nothing. I sat with her cradled in my arms, the edges of the tub scoring lines into my flesh. Still nothing.

The night, achingly slow in its passage, finally turned the shadowed near-light of the hour before dawn. I walked across the parking lot to the motel and opened the door, whistled softly, and waited for Dexter's soft thud as he dropped from the bed to the floor and padded over to greet me, his nose cool in my hand. The grass behind the motel was wet with dew, and it was silent except for Dexter snuffling in the grass. Even the big trucks stopped running for this hour.

I didn't know how I was going to continue, but I thought of Susan, enjoying love for maybe the first time in her life. And I thought of my mother and her nostalgia for those happiest years of her life. And I thought of the love I'd found for Eric and Mickey and how, even though I'd not been the most cheerful of companions, they'd stuck with me and, even through their grief, tried to be upbeat.

They'd been so brave, my little family, living through losses so huge I could hardly imagine them. I could only try and follow, haltingly, in their footsteps, only slide my feet into the footprints they'd dug in the deep snows of their winters, and be thankful they'd been there before me.

The room was cool and still when Dexter and I returned. Neither of the boys moved as I lifted Dexter back onto the bed, but when he'd finished his circling I felt rather than saw them shift slightly so that their bodies, one on each side, touched his.

I sat on the floor beside the bed and closed my eyes, straining to distinguish each boy's breath, the quick light baby breath of Mickey, the stronger, slower exhalations of Eric. I slowed my breathing, matching it to Eric, sleeping in the deep almost-coma of a fifteen-year-old. I felt the exhaustion roll over me, grab me in its embrace until I slept, waking once as the sun first hit the window, then not again until the carts of the maids started rattling by outside the door.

And still the boys slept. I marveled at their ability to sleep through the cacophony of sounds a motel could produce in a single morning. Showers and toilets running and squeaking, smokers hacking their way through the first cigarette of the day. Doors slamming and drivers of diesel trucks revving their cold engines. The rattle of the maids' carts and their cheery voices yelling to one another. Families far better organized than us milling around packing their cars for an early start.

I'd come to anticipate those noises, to look forward to the first of them. They kept me company as I watched the sun move across the sky behind the curtains that never quite shut it out. They gave me something to concentrate on. I spent hours deciphering each sound, placing it into the jigsaw puzzle of morning while I waited for the first movement from the bed. When it came, this morning, oddly, from Eric rather than Mickey, I rolled over away from their bed and headed for the shower.

No motel seemed able to get water pressure right—it was either a dribble or Niagara Falls. While I stood under the needle-sharp spray, I thought about the night I'd survived and the day to come. West Edmonton Mall was Mickey's plan, though what we'd do with Dexter was beyond me. We'd figure it out as we went along, just as we'd been doing.

CHAPTER 10

Beating is an ineffective method for collecting
dragonflies, although some collectors find it sat-
isfying even when no specimens result from its
use. Take a stick and hit the branch hard enough
to shake the insect down on a cloth or tray.
Striking twice helps—once to loosen the insect's hold on the branch, the second time to
shake it loose.
—*The Sunshine Coast News*, September 14, 2005

The road from Hinton to Edmonton wound up and
down hills, through sparse forests (only residents of the
prairies would call them that), past lakes and farms and
ranches. We saw our first grain elevators and our first
oil wells. The country was new to all of us, but even
Mickey's highly honed skills with map and tourist book
found nowhere to stop. Finally we traveled almost as I'd
planned at the beginning—driving mile after mile without distraction, except, of course, for stopping every half

hour or so for one or the other of them to pee or eat or buy another drink. Even so, we made good time.

We arrived in the maze of highways surrounding Edmonton early in the afternoon. The freeways clumped up together like the wires behind my computer and I found myself equally unable to figure out what went where. I froze. The car slowed while I grabbed the map from the dash, although why I thought that would help when even the sight of an unopened computer manual frightened me, was beyond my imagination. I wasn't thinking; I was panicking.

"Where the hell are we? Seventeen A? I don't see that highway anywhere. Which exit is this?"

Around us cars and trucks honked and swerved, creating a little eddy of hysteria in the heretofore peaceful passage of a weekday afternoon. The car slowed even further as I steered erratically and tried to read the map, adding nausea to the panic in the process, both of them welling up like tears at a funeral.

"Shit. Where the hell are we?" And I didn't even worry about the boys hearing me swear. I banged the steering wheel. "Shit. Shit. Shit."

Eric rescued us. He leaned over and pulled the map from my hands. He touched me for the first time in weeks, awkwardly patting me on the shoulder. He spoke in the same voice he used with Dexter, an adult's voice. Strong yet comforting.

"See the sign? The exit to West Edmonton Mall is just up the way. We're almost there."

While I tried to dig us out of the traffic jam I'd created without killing us or anyone else, Eric continued to talk, his voice low and soothing. He pointed out the sights, the exit I needed to take, gave me warnings about upcoming traffic and turns. I was so astonished to hear his voice that I didn't have time to panic, too busy worrying that he might revert to silence as soon as this crisis was over. Worrying about someone else was a good way to curb anxiety. I'd already learned that this trip.

We arrived at West Edmonton Mall in one piece. From the outside, it looked like a huge gray jailhouse. No windows, no trees or grass, only concrete and construction. We parked the car on Floor One of a ten-story parking garage, thus keeping Dexter out of the sun, and carefully noted the number and location.

Mickey said, "All the guidebooks say to remember where you parked. Write it down. They have a whole bunch of guys who work here and all they do is help people find their cars. Cool job, huh?"

"Yeah, if helping lost old guys is your idea of fun."

Eric disparaged the idea but I could see he was interested. He would be sixteen in the fall and more than anything else in the world he wanted his driver's license and his own vehicle. And that meant a job.

Susan wanted him to concentrate on school; Eric

wanted a truck. Immovable object meets mission impossible force. I had my money on Eric. He told me, when we were still talking, that he needed a truck for two reasons. The girls would love it, though I didn't know why he was worried about that. They already loved him. Tall, well-built, gorgeous. Smart and funny. If I was twenty years younger, I'd love him too. He had girls coming out his ears. Kelly, Rita, Shirl, Franny, Lisa. There were so many I couldn't keep track.

But the second reason, he said, was the important one. He needed a truck to get out of the city and up into the mountains so he could paint. Wilderness, not gardens. And when I saw him with the pictographs, I understood exactly what he meant. When we got home, I would tell Susan, show her the photographs I had taken, so she would understand as well. Eric was an artist right down to the bone and she was going to have to live with that or lose him.

Dexter whined as we walked away from the car, but Eric had given him a pep talk, a bowl of water and a handful of doggie treats, so he refrained from barking. One of us would come back every couple of hours to mop up the spilled water and take him for a walk, but he was fine for now, curled up on one of Mickey's T-shirts.

I laid the ground rules as we walked through the cavernous parking lot. One of us had to be the still center at all times, an anchor for the others. I expected most times it would be me, but if I wanted to look at something, one of them would have to take my place. We'd touch base every hour on the hour. I checked to make sure they were both wearing their watches.

"Mine says two o'clock. What about yours?" Mickey loved the idea of synchronizing our watches.

"It's not two o'clock, it's just after one."

"No, no, no. Randy, we're in Alberta, remember? Didn't you see the sign? You were supposed to turn your watch ahead at the border."

He looked at me with the exact expression I'd seen on men my whole adult life, the expression that says, *Don't be such an idiot, hon*. It's a combination of love and disbelief at the depths of idiocy to which women stoop. Mickey had it down pat. Sometimes, when I was with Eric and Mickey, I understood exactly why all my dates were so difficult. They'd never grown out of the exasperating habits they'd acquired as teenagers, when they believed, without any doubt, that they were God's gift to the world. When a man or a teenage boy speaks to you in that tone, with the implied *hon* at the end of the sentence, there's nothing to be done but nod and adjust your watch.

"It's two o'clock. We'll aim for on-the-hour. It's easier to remember, okay?"

Two nods, but I could tell they were already gone.

The chances of getting through the day without one of us getting lost were so remote I simply steeled myself to the idea and got prepared to look for them at some point.

We walked out of the concrete jungle and into a world filled with light and color and noise. Mostly noise, overwhelming, at least to me, but the boys' faces lit up the minute the doors opened. It reminded me of the days when they were little and I took them to the PNE parade. They sat, awestruck on the curb, as motorcycle drill teams, floats, bands, horses and clowns passed by. And it didn't matter how tacky the floats were, or how out of tune the bands, or how long the parade continued, their faces never lost that look.

After we'd scoped out the place, I ordered a conference.

"Time for a break. Something to eat and drink."

I didn't care about the boys, but I was dying for a cup of tea and my stomach felt like I'd forgotten I had one.

"Okay, so where do we go from here?" I asked the question even though I already knew the answer.

"The rides."

"I'll go take Dexter for a walk, and I'll meet you there." I handed over enough money for a day pass. I knew we'd be there for the rest of the day, with maybe a few detours for sustenance.

Dexter was delighted to see me, his doggy breath rancid on my face. It broke his heart, and mine when, after a short walk, I put him back in the car. My pep talk was far less effective than Eric's. I heard Dexter's poor-abandoned-me bark all the way to the door of the mall.

The rides and midway inhabited their own small world sans glitter, except of their own making. The walls were the same unpainted and unfinished concrete as the exterior but pieces of rides, roller coasters, Tilt-A-Whirls and pirate ships were all piled on top of each other, a crazy quilt whirlygig attached to the walls and ceilings with the most precarious-looking cables. The whole room, if something so huge could be called a room, looked like a Lego construction, built by an incredibly smart six-year-old without the slightest idea of or concern for how things should be put together.

The floor trembled. I felt it up my legs and through my groin, where it dispersed, leaving me slightly shaken. Had it really been so long? Obviously. Because when the roller coaster roared past me a second time, the same thing happened. A wave of nostalgia rolled over me, for the feel of a man's body, for the comfort and seldom experienced (at least by me) but never forgotten joy that came with making love with someor you cared for and who cared for you back.

The nostalgia pissed me off. I'd felt it before, usu just before I got involved with another loser. I di want that to happen again. I needed something to tract me from the messages my body was sending. And I needed it in a hurry.

I spun in a circle, checking the dozens of distractions—rides, which made me sick; video games, which basically served to remind me of what a klutz I was; feats of strength and skill, which made me recognize how little of either I had. But I tried anyway. One roller coaster, the smallest one, half-an-hour recovery time lying on the bench at the exit trying not to vomit. Pac-Man, sixty seconds start to finish. Me dead, all the bad guys laughing their heads off at my lack of chomp-power. I tried the Ferris wheel, no recovery time but no distraction either, too slow and filled with couples cuddled up on the red Naugahyde benches above and below me. Teenage couples, honeymooners, bent-over farmers with their sun-wrinkled wives. The slight motion of the Ferris wheel kept my hormones pumping, while the loneliness of sitting on that bench by myself reignited the nostalgia. And then I found it.

Surrounded by silence, no children within twenty feet, a waist-high box with a huge rubber mallet attached by a chain to the top of it. No neon lights or flashing signs, just a picture of a generic kind of animal peeking up out of the earth, and the words Whack-A-Mole.

The moles—brown and shapeless, adorned with yellow eyes and painted-on teeth—randomly popped out f a dozen holes sawed into the top of the box. The whackee—that was me—raised the rubber mallet and hit the moles on their little rubber heads, making them vanish back into their holes with a satisfyingly loud crunch.

I whacked the moles, left-handed first, then right, then settled into a two-handed stance, slightly crouched at the knees. I crashed 'em. Smashed 'em. Banged 'em. Wolloped 'em. I hit those damn plastic moles a thousand times, until my arms ached and my teeth too, from clenching them. And then I whacked 'em some more. Each time I made contact, I felt better; each time I missed, I became more determined to get the little bugger the next time. I left only to replenish my cache of quarters. Both the nostalgia and the longing were almost gone. But I couldn't step away; I just kept whacking, again and again and again. Satisfaction. Pain. The bliss of an endorphin rush. I was hooked.

Eric pried the mallet from my hands and took my arm. He looked alarmed at the smile on my face. I didn't blame him. I couldn't see it, but I felt it and it felt unlike any other smile I'd ever worn. When I passed the mirrored columns on the way out of the midway I caught a glimpse of myself wearing Jack Nicholson's smile from *The Shining*.

The boys sat me down and ordered cowboy-sized burgers and fries and even remembered to order me a diet Pepsi instead of whatever sugar-loaded drink they were having. Halfway through the burger, I spoke.

"So," I said, "have you had enough?"

"Can we come back on our way home?" Mickey always negotiated before he answered.

"If we return this way." I was on to him. Because Mickey never forgot anything. Ever. If I promised a treat for his birthday, even six months in advance, he'd remind me. But he was fair, too, and wouldn't hound me if we came home via the southern route.

"Eric?"

He only nodded, but I didn't care. Each day he spoke more, as if he couldn't help himself, as if the combination of Dexter's enthusiasm and my inability to cope were forcing him to take charge.

"Then let's go get Dexter." I wrapped the remainder of my burger in a napkin and pulled a plastic bag from my purse with a shock of recognition. My mother had performed that same simple action every time we went out to eat, and I had hated her for embarrassing me in public. I looked over at Eric and Mickey but they remained oblivious.

I shook off the feeling of déjà vu and followed the boys to the car. Time to take Dexter for a walk, time to navigate the busy streets of Edmonton and find a motel that would take the whole family.

Mickey bounced, Eric loped, and I took up the rear,

each of us scrutinizing the signs to make sure we were headed the right way. With the three of us working together, we'd find the car, the motel, and the road out of town for the next stage of our journey. No problem.

Eric's Notebook West Edmonton Mall

Big deal. We had to leave Dexter in the car all day while we were inside pretending to have fun. Well, I pretended. I think Mickey and Randy really did have a good time.

Randy loved that stupid mole game. She didn't even shake afterward. I promised myself I'd do whatever Mickey wanted and that I wouldn't fight with him all day. So I followed him on and off the roller coaster thirty-two times. The first couple of times were kind of cool, but thirty-two times? He had fun, though, I could see it.

He wouldn't go by himself, not even at the end. So I kept going. You can't talk on the roller coaster; it takes all your attention just to breathe. I started watching the shapes and colors. They'd make a cool painting. I took some pictures and I'll try and paint it. If we ever get home, that is.

I hate having people around all the time. It makes me tired.

CHAPTER 11

Every decent laborer also has his garden, which
is half his support, as well as his delight.
—Gilbert H. White

The house was definitely going to kill him. Their
love-at-first-sight relationship quickly degenerated into
name-calling on his part and bouts of cheap practical
jokes, mostly on hers. He knew the house was female,
her gender obvious from the first day. Because, of
course, he had fallen in love, and once in that state, he
couldn't get out. He had no experience to fall back on,
no way to know that falling out of love could be just as
easy as falling in once you put your mind to it.

Tom Webb was not a stupid man. He had a Ph.D. in
botany, for heaven's sake, plus assorted undergraduate
degrees, including one in psychology—chosen before
he realized he was a complete chump at human inter-
action—and a couple in pure science. He had shifted
to science when he realized he wasn't even that good

at interacting with animals. But give him a tree or a shrub or a plant and he was a genius.

So Tom took scientific steps to solve his problem with the house. He was convinced, first of all, that most of the near accidents were bids on her part for attention. His attention. So he lavished her with it. He talked to her, even decided to give her a name, although the name itself was a matter of luck more than anything else. He wandered into the library, got a book of baby names from the shelf, and held it out for the librarian.

"Pick one," he said. "I need a name for a girl."

Her eyes, behind the cat's-eye glasses, glittered with something he chose to regard as amusement. Tom was convinced this woman, whose name tag read Mona Charles, was a clone of the world's perfect librarian. He assumed they had found the pattern, after long and arduous combing through libraries all over the globe, in some small midwestern town where all the houses wore front porches and rocking chairs, where all the men wore suits and hats and came home for dinner to a wife who did volunteer work and kids whose idea of trouble was egging doors on Halloween. Dinner, roast or meat loaf, mashed potatoes and gravy, appeared on the table at five-thirty each night. Teenagers still took their homework to the library and the original Mona Charles was a good friend to all of them.

Tom believed in librarians, in their ability to know

what was needed. As a lonely and confused child he had spent a lot of time in the neighborhood library. Mrs. Milyan watched him for weeks and then one day, without ever having said a word to him except, "These books are due back in two weeks," and "Don't mark the pages," and he having said even less, she handed him a book.

"I think you'll like this one, Tom Webb."

And he did. It was full of pictures of trees and plants and shrubs, full of lovely sing-songy Latin names, full of complicated yet perfectly understandable—if, that is, you were Tom Webb and you were paying attention—descriptions of genus and growing patterns and propagation rules. Tom was hooked.

Each night for two weeks he lay in bed after lights out, the covers over his head, his flashlight in hand. He loved the photographs, loved the names, but mostly he loved the stories about the men who discovered and named these beautiful things. He wanted a new species named after him; he wanted that more than anything else in the world.

So at a time when his peers were starting to notice girls, to learn their names and habits, Tom turned to flora. That's what he always called it, to himself and to others, his love of growing things, the name sweet in his mouth like wild strawberries. Fragaria. He spent his weekends taking the bus downtown to the botanical gardens or out to the outskirts of the city to collect specimens, ever hopeful of finding and identifying something new, never before seen. Even a weed, though to a botanist, he discovered, there was no such thing as a weed, would be a start. And he became more and more isolated. But he didn't care, flora was enough for him.

All of this ran through his head while he waited for Mona Charles to name his house.

"Rosamunde," she said, and Tom nodded.

"Rosamunde. What does it mean? Who was she?"

She handed him the book. It opened, without prompting, to the right page. Tom had expected nothing less. All librarians had supernatural powers and this clone of the perfect librarian would have more than most.

He read the lines out loud.

"'From the Latin. Pure rose. She was the mistress of Henry II, king of England in the twelfth century. She was murdered by his wife, Queen Eleanor.'"

Mona Charles said, "I like to think of the name as Rose of the World. Rose Munde. Two separate words. Will that do?"

"I thank you. My poor sore head thanks you. My house, who now has a name, a beautiful name, thanks you."

Tom bowed, exposing the bandage right in the center of his bald spot. Yesterday, Rosa Munde had somehow managed to shut a window, one which the day before had taken him almost two hours to pry out of its paint-encrusted frame, right on top of his head. This was added to lost tools—Tom was fanatically neat with his tools, each with its own place and he always, when he finished with one, wiped it and put it away—and unfindable drafts and invisible people dropping invisible things throughout the house, leaving dents in the hardwood floors. It was all too much for Tom. He hoped giving her a name would stop these things from happening.

He raced home to his Black & Decker Workmate with an excruciatingly expensive four-foot slab of black maple he had bought at the lumberyard. He took his pencil and drew the letters of her name onto the wood, measuring the spacing and the height, erasing and rewriting the letters a dozen times to get it right. He used simple script, plain and elegant.

It was almost dark by the time he picked up the router and began the slow, painstaking task of gouging out the wood around the letters of her name—Rosa Munde—two separate words just as Mona Charles had suggested. The letters stood out sharp and clear in the harsh, stark shadows cast by the arc lights over the Workmate.

Tom stepped back, tilted his head first to the right, then to the left. In the morning he would walk down to the hardware store after breakfast and pick out some brass chain and fasteners to attach the name to the front porch. Was there anything else he could do to make the sign more beautiful? Stain the wood around the letters but not the letters themselves. They would stand out. He would buy the stain in the morning. He stretched his back, sore from hunching over the sign for hours, and realized he hadn't eaten since lunch.

The fridge was full because Tom liked to cook, enjoyed experimenting with flavors and textures. He thought one day he might write a cookbook. But tonight he was too tired to do anything more than slap peanut butter and his homemade raspberry jam between two slices of bread and eat it while he walked through the house on his nightly tour. It wasn't an inspection, exactly, more of an appraisal. What he'd done that day, what he planned for the next, what felt urgent, what not.

Tom Webb, having for most of his life been a man of rules and lists and order, had arrived in Cranberry Portage prepared to continue in that fashion. His lists were printed in large black letters, starting with what logic decreed to be most urgent. But all logic had deserted him when he entered the house. The lists were still there, pinned to the wall above his workbench, but instead of using his thick red Magic Marker to eliminate tasks, one by one, from the top to the bottom, the lists looked like a crazy quilt. He added things, inserted them in the middle, did things without even putting them on the list. There was no rhyme or reason to his progress.

He did something each day, each task determined almost at random during his nightly walk-through. Each morning he worked on whatever had grabbed his attention the night before. It was slow and disorganized. Most of all it was fun. It involved almost daily trips downtown to pick up supplies.

Tom became a fixture in that one block of Main Street. He haunted the library, the hardware store, the tiny general market. He drove out of town to the lumberyard at least once a week. But his home away from home was the Coffee Shop, name following function. He didn't eat there much—he preferred his own cooking to the greasy fare provided there—but he consumed countless cups of crummy coffee and quickly became part of the town's life and gossip chain. Because he was a newcomer, everyone who entered the Coffee Shop eventually joined him at the booth in the window. They quizzed him about his past, his marital status, his house, his future.

Maude Fowler, town clerk and chief busybody, was the worst inquisitor, but also the most informative. She knew everything and everybody. Not just the current residents, but everyone who'd ever lived in Cranberry Portage. Tom was convinced she had every single file in the Town Hall memorized, all the way back to the beginning. If she walked by the window and spotted Tom, she abandoned whatever errand she'd been on to join him and continue her interrogation. Tom didn't mind much, she reminded him of his mother.

Besides, she told him more than she learned. He consoled himself with that thought after he'd told her things he'd told no one else, like how he came to buy the house. Tom's life had been, until he first saw Rosa Munde, about as boring as oatmeal without brown sugar and raisins, but he loved the stories Maude told him. Especially about Rosa Munde's history.

Maude told him the house never had a name.

"It's just the MacLean house, always has been. Didn't need to know more than that. Only got an address a couple of years ago. Even Ben Roman didn't give it a name."

Maude looked at him over the rims of her bifocals. *Who are you*, those faded blue eyes seemed to say. *Who are you to change tradition?*

"She needed a name." Tom defended himself. "And I gave her a beautiful one. Rosa Munde. Rose of the World."

Tom felt as if he were back in first grade, bringing home his first piece of art to his mother. She had to like it, she just had to.

"Ha." But Maude's face softened a little. "My mother's name was Rose."

Not unqualified approval, Tom thought, but it would do to be going on with.

The house sat silent on its leaf-strewn knoll. The

yard, except for the flat shelf at the top where the house sat like a queen on her throne, sloped down to the street at the front and to the Cranberry River at the back. If there was grass, it lay buried beneath years of leaf mold, each fall another layer settling comfortably on top of the last. It was a mess. Tom stepped off the paving stones he'd carefully replaced in the path up to the front porch and sank into a foot of mulch. Too bad he didn't have time for a garden this summer. Perfect compost material.

Tom had decided last night that today was the day to strip the wallpaper in the kitchen, but he realized as soon as he felt the spring air cool and clean on his face that he needed a break from the house. He'd spent weeks inside. It was time to do something about the yard.

Snowshoes were probably the only thing that might have made his sloshing journey to the outbuildings easy. But his were still in Winnipeg, in storage with everything else he'd deemed superfluous to the summer's work. He planned a trip to the city before snowfall and would pick them up then. How could he have known they'd come in handy in May? He shook his head and kept sloshing.

There were three outbuildings. One obviously a garage, which he ignored. His truck could stay outside until the fall. The other two, though, either one of them might contain gardening tools. He couldn't imagine Mrs. Roman packing those. Maude had made it clear that the Romans took only what fit in their station wagon with Mrs. Roman, Susan and the other girl. All the furniture had been sold at auction.

"Almost everyone in town has a piece of that house in their living room or den or bedroom. I have the bedroom suite that the original Josh MacLean brought from Toronto in a buggy. Ask around. They'll be happy to tell you."

Lloyd: "I bought the dining-room suite. I was just getting married and I thought it'd impress Julie. It did. She still hates it."

Mona the librarian: "They donated their books to the library. Some of them are still on the shelf. Especially Ben's books. They're like new. No one ever looks at them. But all the girls' books are gone now, read to death."

Tom made a note to himself to take Ben's books out of the library, to take them home to Rosa Munde and see what she thought of them. Mona would know which ones they were, even though she'd acquired them over thirty years ago.

Mona again: "And I couldn't resist the plant stands for myself. They're mahogany."

Everyone had taken something and was delighted to tell him about it. So Tom walked through the town looking at the houses with a little singsong verse in his head.

Fireplace irons.
Laundry tub.
Sofa, chairs and hassock.
Dining table.
Many chairs.
Hat stand made of maple.

He felt as if the life of the house had been shattered by this scattering of her possessions. She needed him to bring her back to herself and cleaning up the yard would help. No one had mentioned gardening tools. They might be a bit rusty but he'd find them in one of the buildings.

A peculiar sharp odor hung over the outbuildings, familiar, but Tom didn't know from where. Dead mice? Squirrels? Some kind of mold? He thought about leaving the yard for another day but he was in the mood and the weather was perfect. Cool, dry, sunny.

"Do it, Tom. How bad can it be?" Talking himself into it, he kicked at the dead bolt hanging limply from the rotted frame of the nearest building.

"Shit."

The building erupted with noise and what felt like thousands of tiny black bodies squeaking in a pitch almost too high for Tom to hear. He fell back, swatting at his head and face and hair. The odor, sharp and unpleasant, welled up out of the door, enveloping him. The bodies disappeared as if by magic. They were there, scaring his heart out of his chest and then they were gone, leaving only their smell behind. He recognized it now, of course. Bat guano. Lots and lots and lots of bat guano. A whole room's worth. Years' worth. Hundreds of generations' worth.

He picked himself up off the ground and brushed the dead leaves from his clothes. He circled the outbuilding, noting the broken window allowing the bats' entry. Fixing that was now at the top of the things-to-do list. The second building looked secure, no broken glass, no holes in the roof, no misaligned doors.

He peered through the filthy window into the shadowy depths of the small space. Nothing. He saw nothing. He rattled the door. No response. No noise. No chittering of tiny squeak-voiced bats. But this padlock, rust and all, resisted his kicks. Tom resorted to the pick on his Swiss Army knife. No padlock could stand up to that, given steady hands and plenty of time. His hands weren't so steady but he persevered, pausing often to check over his shoulder, anticipating the return of the bats.

His hands shook, but eventually the padlock yielded, though the hair on the back of his neck was permanently erect by the time he opened the door. Dusty. Not damp. Plenty of cobwebs. No bats.

The tools were stored in the way he would do so himself. Neatly hung from the walls, from smallest to largest. They'd been clean when they were put away and when he touched the blades, he felt no creeping stain of rust.

He picked up the rake. It came into his hands as if he'd owned it forever, as if the grooves worn into the handle had been made by his hands. He touched the other tools: a hoe, a shovel, a trowel. Each of them settled comfortably into his palms.

A lawn mower huddled in the corner next to a gas can. No need to look at that. There would be no living grass under the layers of mulch, but Tom stood for a moment, contemplating the yard as it must have been the day Ben Roman put his tools away for the last time. An emerald green lawn, pruned and tidy fruit trees, a lush rose garden. There would be rosebushes waiting somewhere in the mess. And he would bring them back to life.

He shouldered the rake and the shovel, then had second thoughts and threw them into the wheelbarrow. Tom marched back out into the sun. The job of clearing the yard was a huge one, but he'd make a start and do a little bit every day. And then he'd have a bonfire, a big one, starting with the leaves, throwing on all the bits and pieces he'd ripped out of the house. Everyone would see the flames. He looked forward to that.

CHAPTER 12

All insects require the right conditions to grow. Dragonflies need water for the first (larval or nymph) stage and wide open spaces for the adult (imago) stage of their lives. Digging a pond in your yard will attract dragonflies and, quick to recognize a new habitat, will soon colonize your yard.
—*The Sunshine Coast News*, September 14, 2005

We were late. We were very, very late. I sounded like the White Rabbit but I felt more like Alice, disappearing into a world where everything was uncontrolable, especially myself. Every day a new me appeared, an unexpected aspect of myself, as if I, like Alice, ate or drank something, a mushroom, a pill, a syrup, and thus changed my life completely. But unlike Alice, my changes were internal. And I wasn't going to wake to find I'd been dreaming in the sun.

It was all too real for that. Maybe that was the problem, the onslaught of reality. Unhappy boys, crazy dog, candy wrappers, pop cans, rock music, a sick sister, the endless prairie road. And hundreds of bugs on the windshield, all of which should have been gobbled up by the hundreds of red-tailed hawks on the fence posts next to the highway.

I'd spent most of my life not exactly ignoring reality but bending it to my will. If a boyfriend dumped me, before long I would be the one who had dumped him. My job wasn't a fluke. I'd planned to be a banker, knowing that women were becoming more and more likely to break through the glass ceiling. I was single by choice, stuck at home by choice, working my way up the corporate ladder by choice. If things stayed still, if I hadn't taken this trip, I would have found a way to turn my layoff into choice.

"I needed a break," I'd say. "Time for me to change careers, do something more exciting, maybe even creative," even though the most creative thing I'd done in my life had been to paint a few already molded plaster cups, which turned out to be so ugly even Susan threw hers away.

"And getting all that severance pay will help me change my life, give me time to contemplate my move." Translation: I was shit-scared, had no idea what I was going to do, and it might take me a year to get the courage to go on a single interview.

This trip was peeling away those layers of subterfuge

and leaving me with the damned truth. And that pissed me off. Reality was too gruesome for me, coping with it too difficult. This summer, though, I was without options. Something about it—the long hours in the car, the continual presence of the boys, my mother in the trunk—conspired against my ascent into my regular highly fictionalized life.

Perhaps the biggest difference was my inability to escape into books. They'd always been my solace. When I read a book, I went somewhere else, and by the time I returned, the world had reinvented itself. Or I reinvented it. Didn't matter which, the result was the same. I could cope. That was impossible now when I couldn't even open a book.

Before we set off on this adventure, I had estimated five days to Cranberry Portage, yet more than a week in, we were still two provinces away. The panic which until now I'd been able to contain, at least in the daylight, welled up whenever I stopped concentrating on the road in front of me or the lyrics from the Discman next to me or the dog and boy roughhousing in the back seat.

I kept getting lost in the prairie sky, even after I'd become aware of the danger. I'd be driving along, watching the road, halfheartedly counting the hawks with Mickey and waiting for the next yellow splotch to commit suicide on my windshield, when I'd look up and eternity would grab me.

The pale-blue summer sky extended past what I knew of the world. I expected horizon, I anticipated an ending. On these plains, there was neither. The sky went on forever, curving to meet the road in front of me and doing exactly the same in the road visible in the rearview mirror. There was no way to fix myself in the landscape, nothing to act as anchor. If I let go, I would float up and disappear into the blue. All the clichés of the prairie sky—the huge blue bowl of it, the endlessness, the size and shape of it—were unbelievably, accurately true. And it scared me.

I added nausea and agoraphobia to my panic attacks. I was a walking encyclopedia of mental illnesses. I didn't know until I hit the center of Alberta that it was possible to be as sick as I obviously was and still function. For the first time in the years since the onset of my anxiety, I began to wonder if it was an indicator of something more serious, if it led to panic attacks, to agoraphobia, and then what? Manic-depressive illness? Schizophrenia? Multiple personality disorder? Compulsive-obsessive disorder? ADD?

The first three seemed more than possible; they seemed probable, maybe inevitable. I had, since the beginning of the trip, felt like at least two people. Daytime and nighttime. Sometimes, while the sun still shone on the mountains, I felt like my old in-control self, but since our expulsion from the soothing deep green of the forest, that momentary reassurance had vanished, along with the color green in any of its recognizable forms.

The prairies abhorred green, at least that's how it felt this far into the summer. Yellow and gold and the palest of beige predominated. A few fields flaunted cornflower blue, a few spindly trees tried to buck the trend, but their greenery was insufficient to have any effect other than to remind me of what I missed. The sense I'd had of being pegged out on a flat, hot desert returned in spades. Exposed. Every single inch of me.

Driving into the haze of the afternoon sun, I felt as if someone had skinned me and put my skin back on inside out, so that each bump in the road, each flash of light as the sun hit the windshield of an oncoming car, each hot swirl of desert-dry air from the open window hit me like a hammer. And it hurt. From the minute I walked out of the motel in the morning and got in the car until the sun set at night. We were past the summer solstice and the days wore on forever.

I remembered thinking, trapped in the depths of the mountain valleys, how much I missed the lingering sunsets of the Coast. Now, here on this empty slab of land, I wished them over. The light persisted long into the night and once the sun itself vanished, remnants of it stayed in the sky, long streaks of translucent color, afterlight, still and cold and clear. No matter how long

I sat on the curb in front of the motel, no matter how desperately I wished those reminders away they remained through the night, as if the day had chosen to leave behind a small part of itself, a hint of its power in this place.

The day had no need to worry. I couldn't forget it. That huge yellow eye followed me. I knew it was trying to tell me something, something I didn't understand, and yet another thing I couldn't talk about. The journey, begun so openly, was turning into a quagmire of secrets. I couldn't tell Susan about my panic attacks. Or about the boys' fighting. Or that I spent most nights talking to my dead mother. I couldn't tell her about the progression into nausea and agoraphobia and I definitely couldn't tell her about the sun-eye following me.

Conversations with her might have become impossible except that she was so happy with Steve and her treatment was going so well, she didn't even notice what a mess I was. I wasn't so sure about the boys.

The fighting, down to a dull roar for a few days after we adopted Dexter, was back up to full volume. They fought whenever they ended up within ten feet of each other and on this trip that was most of the time. The only breaks were in the car. Eric had his music; Mickey had Dexter. And the prairie landscape continued to overwhelm me.

We were heading east—not directly, never directly. Cranberry Portage was east, a long way east and slightly north of Edmonton, but we were driving south on our way to Drumheller and the dinosaur museum. Susan mentioned it, plus both Eric and Mickey pretended to remember it from the last time they'd been this way— ten summers ago. Eric maybe, he'd been six, but Mickey? No way.

But he came up with the most corroborative detail. I thought I knew what he was remembering. Just as with the photographs Auntie Mabel had shown me of my father and I together, Mickey jumbled memory and its photographic image together to create his own reality.

Before I'd been to England, I had no real memories of my father. I manufactured them, memories of him holding me, telling me he loved me, taking me for walks, or out in the canoe. I knew them to be fantasies, something along the line of "I'm really a princess adopted by these commoners but some day soon the king, my father, will come to rescue me." As I grew up, I abandoned those fantasies although the memory of them, the way they felt to me, remained.

When I went to England, though, and saw the photographs my father had sent to his sister, they came back to me as if they'd never left, stronger and more complete, now more accurate. I saw the photos, touched his face with my finger, feeling the thick glossy coating on the old pictures on my fingertips. The crinkled edges, the stark black-and-whiteness, the squareness of the images, brought home the reality of them.

They seemed truer than the colored snapshots I took now. But of course, over time, I forgot those images, replacing them with my manufactured memories of the events they represented. And that's what I suspected Mickey had done. The photographs of that trip with his father were part of his memory, not the events themselves.

But for me that distinction was irrelevant. Because now my memories of my father, once absolute fantasy, were backed up with images, real ones, and so they had the power of reality behind them.

Mickey and Eric even consented to get up early— ten o'clock rather than noon—so we could get on the road in time to be in Drumheller for the night, ready to get to the museum as soon as it opened. Edmonton to Drumheller was a big, big day for us, five hours of driving. The road headed out of the city and straight into the country. No transition, no time to become accustomed to the new world we were to travel.

We were in the city and then we crossed an invisible border between civilization and stark land. A duty-free shop might have helped, a couple of customs guards, a stop sign, a barrier. Anything to give me warning of the shock to come.

This was land stripped to the bones, not precisely flat, but boundless. And every dip and dimple, the slightest hint of elevation, all visible. More than that, really. A ten-foot bump in this land had more visual impact than a four-thousand-foot mountain back home. I felt like a voyeur watching the land roll by, everything exposed. It waited for something, I felt sure of that. And of course it made me nervous.

So I encouraged Mickey's chatter about the badlands, the hoodoos, the dinosaurs. Anything to stop the nervousness from shifting up a notch into panic, then fear. Anything to enable me to keep going. Anything to stop me from pulling over to the side of the road and running, screaming, into the wheat fields.

I tugged at Eric's headphones, a liberty unthinkable except in these desperate circumstances.

"Take them off and tell me about the museum."

He hesitated, but I knew he had been watching me carefully and I assumed he saw the desperation I couldn't hide. He pulled off the earphones and, instead of leaving them dangling around his neck ready to put back on, he packed them into their carrying case and put them on the floor at his feet. At that moment I loved this boy-man more than I'd loved anyone or anything in my life.

"It's cool," he said, "and dark."

It took me a moment to distinguish between teen-speak and temperature.

"Even in the summer?"

"Yeah, you walk in from the parking lot and it's hot, no shade, sun beating down on the rocks and pavement. Then you walk in the door into a kind of tunnel, dark, cool, no windows. Cool."

Teen-speak that time.

"The best part is the Tyrannosaurus Rex." That was Mickey. "And the Velociraptors."

"You like the ones with teeth?" I questioned.

"Yeah, and the bigger the better. Forget the baby dinosaurs."

Baby dinosaurs? Where did they get those? I was prepared to be disappointed. The car rolled on through the plains while the boys argued, amicably for once, over dinosaurs and displays. I knew neither of them could remember in such detail. The ghost of Jurassic Park was looming over almost everything Mickey said.

"Maybe this time they'll have live ones. What do you think?"

Eric laughed. "You idiot, they can't do that."

"Why not?"

"Because."

"Because why?"

"Because that was a movie. And we'd have seen it on the news. Remember the sheep? Dolly? A dinosaur would be big news."

"Oh, yeah." Mickey's face fell but only for moment. "Look. Look. Look!" Pointing out the window.

We'd all been disillusioned at the lack of animals in the mountains. But now here they were. Llamas, bison, camels, wolves, and a few other bedraggled animals stood in a series of small, dirty cages. Thirty dollars and two hours later we returned to the car and Dexter, all of us hungry and the three humans rife with the scent of confined, wild animals. All of them tame enough to touch and we petted every single one of them, except I skipped the wolves. They made me uncomfortable, their yellow intelligent eyes offering only a very limited forbearance.

Dexter was so excited by the combination of our return and the exciting aromas we bore with us that he promptly added the odor of dog urine to the pungent reek in the car.

Drumheller was going to have to wait. We needed showers and food and I wasn't going to drive for any longer than absolutely essential, not surrounded by a stench so foul we might as well have an excited skunk in the car.

We were late. We were very, very late. A few hours wasn't going to make the slightest bit of difference.

Eric's Notebook Drumheller

I remember the dinosaur museum. We went there with Dad before he left. I wonder what he's doing now? I don't really miss him but the trip to the museum was fun. Maybe the only time we had fun together. Yeah, 'cause he's an ass.

I liked the lab the best. Watching them make dinosaur bones out of rock. That's what it looked like. I saw one guy take a big yellowy rock and chip away at it until it turned into a jaw and teeth. Like a sculptor. That's what I thought he was.

I want to draw in there. The way the bones reflect in the mirrors. That's cool. They look more real there than they do in real life. I'll tell Randy and maybe she'll take Mickey and leave me alone in the dark for a couple of hours.

But what about Dexter? We have to find shade for him. If there isn't any I'll have to stay outside. We can't leave him in the car in the hot sun. He'll die.

Mum sounded tired last night.

CHAPTER 13

Dragonflies have been around approximately 300 million years, even longer than dinosaurs, and are virtually unchanged from that time. They have survived where dinosaurs have not— through ice ages, volcanoes, even a planet-changing meteor impact. Fossils of dragonflies can be recognized as far back as the Carboniferous period, continuing right through to the present.
—*The Sunshine Coast News*, September 14, 2005

We fell into a fissure in the earth. Shades of Alice. We'd been driving along, the endless view, the red-tailed hawks, Mickey's dragonflies killing themselves against the windshield, when it happened—a long steep slide into another world.

The horizon narrowed to arm's length. The washed-out blue prairie sky darkened as if someone had placed a pane of tinted glass over the cliffs, and we'd become specimens in a zoo or an ant farm. I wanted to call the sky azure, though I had no idea what color that name signified. Azure. It popped into my mind and wouldn't leave, like the last song I heard on the radio in the morning, the one that echoed in my mind all day, the one I'd catch myself singing at the oddest times, always off-key, and with made-up words because I never remembered more than one line of any song.

Some families were musical, some weren't. We—Mum, Susan and me—weren't. My mother joined the Sweet Adelines one year because she saw them in a mall, all dressed up, perfect hair and makeup, and she wanted to take advantage of their grooming knowledge. Maybe she thought she'd get a deal on Avon or at the Beauty Barn.

It was one of the most embarrassing moments of my life. I already felt fragile (that was how my mother put it when she felt bad and needed an extra drink or two before dinner). My periods were painful and flowing like Niagara Falls. Roy had just dumped me, leaving me with physical feelings I didn't know how to deal with.

None of the books I'd read talked about masturbation and, although normally a fast learner, that particular relief eluded me. I was scared all the time. Scared to look at myself, let alone touch. My mother, too open in most ways, didn't believe in sex. Not talking about it, anyway. Certainly not to me.

I imagined my conversation with Susan that night.

"Did she talk to you about sex?" I would have to blurt it out before I lost my nerve.

"Are you kidding? Why else would I marry Don? I got pregnant the first time he touched me."

Would I tell her the same thing had happened to me? About the abortion? I couldn't imagine that far, but I kept practicing the first line, running it over in my head until, like those damned songs, it wouldn't go away.

The year of the Sweet Adelines. I was almost thirteen and knew no one; my breasts were my most memorable feature. And then my mother proceeded to make a complete fool of herself. In public. Right in front of my eyes.

Most of her enthusiasms—my mother was a woman of short but intense enthusiasms—were private ones. Crafts, knitting, sewing, leatherwork, jewelry. All expensive, all discreet. Our closets were full of cast-off equipment and half-finished projects. When she died, I transferred those projects to my closets and continued to contemplate completing one or the other of them. Susan laughed when I told her that. The Sweet Adelines represented a new phase in my mother's life. It was the first public moment of embarrassment. It wasn't the last.

They must have been desperate for new members because even I knew my mother couldn't sing. But once she dressed up in the blue satin dress with the white lace collar, once her hair was frosted and set, once she put on her stage makeup, she looked as if she belonged. I allowed myself a moment of hope. I almost believed everything would be okay and let her drag me to their first concert, and sit me, and Susan, in the front row.

What I forgot, the crucial thing that slipped my mind, was that my mother was a chameleon. She could mirror anyone. I'd seen her transform herself a hundred times, from executive secretary to real estate saleswoman to steak-house hostess to tavern waitress. But she still couldn't sing. And I knew, immediately, what she had done in rehearsal—she had pretended to sing.

The minute she opened her mouth I remembered the other times she looked like she knew what she was doing only to be exposed as a fraud. At least I hadn't been there to see the other times. But this time, her voice was all I heard, her face glowing with excitement.

She didn't heed the conductor's slash across her throat, the increasingly desperate tugs from the poor women standing on either side of her. She didn't notice as the entire choir stumbled and then died. She continued to sing, loudly and off-key, while I wished myself anywhere but there. Because of course she'd pointed us out to everyone before the show, smiling and waving and pointing at her two daughters. Everyone knew who we were.

That feeling came back to me as we disappeared into

the chasm. I hated the exposed prairies but the heat and prehistoric landscape of this enclosed valley were almost as bad. I heard the whine growing louder and more uncontrollable in my head. "I want to go home. I want to go home. I want to go home *now*."

Every change in climate, in scenery, in schedule, felt impossible to me. Dumped back into my teens where every decision was crucial, every choice might ruin my life, I couldn't even pick a rest stop anymore without waffling. Should I stop here or wait until the next one? What if the next one's too far away? What if it's dirty? What if it's closed?

The continually changing landscape—piled on top of my altered life—made every moment an ordeal. Falling into yet another new world, I abandoned all pretense of being in charge and let the boys take over. Besides, having landed in this altered landscape, there were plenty of indicators we were headed the right way.

The small town of Drumheller boasted dinosaurs everywhere. Large purple, green, yellow and pink ones. Molded haphazardly from some plasterlike substance, slapped with nonwaterproof paint, then placed in front of a store. Or an insurance office. Or an ice-cream stand. They were unidentifiable unless duplicates of Barney might be considered a species of dinosaur.

I cringed as we drove through the town. I'd expected something more scientifically accurate. The heat, trapped in the valley, rolled over us. It felt as if we were locked in a sauna while someone kept turning up the heat. But the boys didn't seem to notice. All three of us sat in silence, their faces masks of contemplation as they watched this new world. I tried to lift my eyes from the tourist tackiness, to see, as they clearly did, the stark ancient land around us, but the purple plaster dinosaurs and the matching signs—painted by the same person from the same cans of paint—mesmerized me.

The road to the museum led us through and out of town, leaving behind the pudgy dinosaurs and traveling a landscape where we saw only bones, not of dinosaurs though I expected they were there too, but of the earth. Nothing covered them, no dirt or clay, no grass or ground cover, no shrubs or trees. The planet's skeletal structure stood naked to the sun and wind, scraped down to the bone by millions of years of exposure to the elements.

This, then, was the landscape I'd imagined days ago when I saw myself pegged out on the desert floor. Alien yet familiar, it reminded me of something I'd seen, somewhere I'd been in the past. But I knew I'd never been here. Or anywhere like here. Once we left Cranberry Portage my mother, and then I, refused to return to the prairies. I flew over them if I had to get past them to the rest of the world. So why did it feel so familiar? What was I remembering? An image flashed into my mind. John Wayne and those old westerns filmed in black-and-white. Of course I expected cowboys or Indians to appear at the top of the cliffs.

I thought about that for a minute. I shared my mother's hatred of westerns, never watched them, though of course it was impossible not to know of John Wayne, not to recognize his face. But I knew I'd never seen him in a movie, was quite sure I'd never watched a western except for *High Plains Drifter* during the summer of Roy, and all that did was to put me off westerns even further.

"Randy?" A voice from the back seat interrupted my musings. "Pull over at this rest stop. Dexter needs out."

Mickey and Eric had both given up asking me whether it was okay to stop. They told me what to do and I did it. I pulled into the sparse shade cast by the Dumpster behind the washrooms. I turned off the car with a sigh of relief.

"We're going up that cliff. Come on." Dexter and Mickey were already leaping up the hill, but Eric stooped to the window to check.

I shook my head. "You guys go ahead. I'll wait here. It's too hot for me."

I watched them go up the hill, the path white against the yellow cliffs. Black shadows delineated time's depredation, giving depth and an air of meaning to the scene. I read the message but didn't understand it.

Time's inevitable passage? Mortality? The hopelessness of fighting against it? None fit the landscape before me. If anything, it screamed to me of permanence. The lines scored into the earth looked as if they'd always been there, marking some sort of past life.

Those cliffs, their deep indentations, the sparse vegetation as hardy as the pioneers who'd settled the prairies, wouldn't have changed, perhaps since the age of the Albertosaurus. I knew the theories, both Eric and Mickey had gone through the requisite dinosaur phase and I knew more than I'd ever wanted to about dinosaurs and their disappearance. I knew, for instance, that when the dinosaurs inhabited this particular landscape, chances were it looked more like a tropical forest. But I had no trouble imagining the dinosaurs right here, in this sere and stark world.

Right along with John Wayne and his cohorts. I closed my eyes on that thought. The heat enveloped me, pressing into me with the weight of a man, heavy, forcing me into awareness of its presence on every inch of my body. I surrendered to it, to the heat and its resemblance to a man. I slept and in that sleep knew I wore a smile.

But the man who appeared in my dreams wasn't who I expected. No ex-lover, no phantom dream date, but my father. We sat side by side on a couch in a room, which felt familiar though I recognized nothing of it.

It was dark and I was young. I knew things in this dream. I knew that the scene had been enacted many times. It had the feel of ritual.

A yellow plastic bowl—was that popcorn?—and two matching tumblers sat on the coffee table. A glass bottle of Coke accompanied them. I watched my father pour the fizzing pop into the glasses, watched to make sure the contents were equal. He pulled the table closer so we could both reach it, then looked at his watch.

"It's time," he said, and I felt an unmistakable surge of pleasure in response to those words.

I woke just enough to worry about the possibilities inherent in this dream. I returned to it with the added burden of an adult's thoughts and fears.

In the dream I knew what was going to happen and the child in me anticipated it with joy. My time with my father. Mum was upstairs with Susan and it was time for Dad's favorite show. Mum hated it, so after many arguments, she left us alone to enjoy it. Sunday night, seven o'clock, the music swells, the credits roll across the black-and-white screen. *Bonanza*. Hoss and Little Joe, Ben and Adam.

I didn't always understand what happened on the screen, I couldn't have been more than four or five, but it didn't matter. I was with Dad, eating and drinking in the living room—punishable by death any other time of the week—staying up past my bedtime, watching the life of a family as different from ours as it was possible to be.

I woke from the dream a second time. No nagging adult concerns, just a sense of profound joy. I had, at last, one true memory of my father, even if it had come in a dream. The surroundings, familiar and alien at the same time, brought it to me. Because from the things I did know, I knew I hadn't seen *Bonanza*, I also knew the dream to be inspired by a real memory. My mother hated westerns with a passion, and I did, too, though without knowing where her aversion came from. A reminder of another time when my father spent time with me, not her.

Bonanza. The theme song rang in my head. Da da-da da da-da da da da da Bonanza. I couldn't remember the words. What were they? I needed to know.

Suddenly the car felt unbearably hot. I reached into the back for water, ignoring the abyss of garbage my fingers found before closing on the plastic bottles. The water was warm but it tasted like heaven. I rolled up the windows, placed the sunshade in the front windshield and locked the doors behind me.

The path the boys had taken was still and silent. I paused halfway up and looked back down to the parking lot. No cars except mine. Everyone else was smart enough to get out of the midday sun. When I reached the top of the cliff, not far in feet but miles in terms of energy expended, I shaded my eyes and scanned the flat plain for the boys. I heard them before I saw them. Faint yappings, laughs, snatches of words, whispered across the dead grass, swirling around me like tiny tornadoes, the direction impossible to pinpoint.

They had vanished in the heat haze. What I finally saw was a flash of motion rather than a body. They had followed the edge of the cliff around until they stood directly over the museum. Below us raced dinosaurs, grown-up cousins crafted by Michelangelo as opposed to the cartoonists who'd built the pink-and-purple caricatures living in the town. From this distance, enveloped in the heavy air of a summer afternoon, they might have been real.

Eric sat, his feet dangling over the edge (I subdued my shiver of fear), sketchbook in hand, while Mickey and Dexter chased dragonflies behind him.

"Okay, gang. It is way too hot out here." I handed one water bottle to Eric, another to Mickey. "Drink." I poured some water into Dexter's bowl and gingerly crouched next to Eric.

The four of us sat in that high place, masters of the world that lay around us, unchanged and unchanging. Even the museum, long and low and dark, appeared to have been there forever. Dragonflies glittered past, miniature replicas of their monstrous precursors.

"Dragonflies have been around for three hundred

and fifty million years. There used to be one as big as a falcon, and they eat all day, mostly mosquitoes, I think."

That moment of doubt wasn't Mickey. He knew more about insects than Eric did about rock music or I did about lousy boyfriends.

"You think?"

"Yeah, well, I've only started studying them since…"

Since his mom got sick and we started this trip. I knew. It was precisely what I would have done if I'd been able to, lose myself in a book. I envied Mickey his ability to focus on facts and figures.

"They're fast. Some of them can fly forty-five feet per second. Can you believe that?"

"If they're so fast how come they keep getting smooshed on the windshield? They're flying faster than we're driving." Eric turned away from the cliff to look at Mickey.

"I don't know. That's why I've been cataloguing them. Maybe I can figure it out."

"Maybe they're flying away from the hawks. Anyway, it's time to go. I'm starving."

I carefully scooted away from the edge before I stood up. I took one more quick look down at the dinosaurs. Maybe this would be okay. At least it would be air-conditioned. If I got bored, there was always the cafeteria.

CHAPTER 14

Dragonflies are voracious eaters. As larva, they eat tiny water creatures, water fleas and mosquito and mayfly larva. As they grow, they eat small fish, tadpoles, waterbeetles and worms. As adults, they devour hordes of mosquitoes and other small insects, helping control these pest populations.
—*The Sunshine Coast News*, September 14, 2005

The moments of tranquility—the dream, the view out into the prehistoric valley, the hours we spent in the cool dark museum—kept seducing me into believing that things were going to be okay, that I was going to be okay. I started to imagine a good night's sleep, a surcease from the anxiety, a reintegration of my two lives.

But the nights proved me wrong. It took three days to drive from Drumheller to Cranberry Portage. We made few stops other than for the necessities of life. Food, drink, pit stops. That was fine with me. I wanted, more than anything, to get out from beneath the relentless prairie sky. Even the frozen tundra of the north had to be better than the simplistic forms of the prairies.

Eric painted it, seeing beauty in the landscape that eluded me. He captured subtle gradations of color and light invisible to my eyes. In his sketches I almost saw the beauty, but it didn't manifest itself in the real world. It all looked the same to me, as if a four-year-old had slapped two wide undifferentiated swatches of color down on a huge sheet of paper, one a kind of muddy brown, the other faded blue.

Eric seemed happy, or not unhappy anyway, though no more communicative than before. He spoke grudgingly to me and only slightly less so to Mickey. His real conversations were with Dexter, as were Mickey's. Oh, Mickey still chattered away, commenting on the scenery or food or something he'd read in one of his books, but never about anything of consequence.

Dexter became a therapist to all three of us. Mickey whispered to him in the car. Eric talked while trying, unsuccessfully, to teach him to heel and come and fetch. I talked to him—I'd given up talking to my mother although I still took her out of the trunk each night and into the laundromat with me—in that pale gray hour just before dawn.

The boys stopped fighting. Perhaps, like me, they felt the weight of the sky pressing down on them. Or maybe they were tired of being in the car, on the road, away from home, and just wanted to get to wherever we were going.

Somewhere between Drumheller and the middle of Saskatchewan, our roles reversed. I wasn't sure I wanted to arrive at our destination despite being desperate to get out of the prairies, but the boys just wanted to get there. So we drove across the prairies, gobbling up the miles as if they were M&M's, one after another, never stopping until the light began to fade.

This was how I'd planned the trip. Driving ten-hour days, moving through the landscape as if it were only a backdrop to the journey, seeing it as moving pictures, one in the windshield, one on each side of the car, one through the rearview mirror. This was how I imagined road trips, our heads bobbing in the car, the world changing around us, but never becoming part of that world, never stepping outside our enclosed aluminum shell into that big unknown space outside.

Now we raced across the prairies, doing precisely what I'd wanted from the beginning, and I was still unhappy.

We stopped for the night in a small Saskatchewan town. There were plenty of motels visible but they were full of pipeline workers—welders and electricians and engineers, laborers and executives—policing and repairing the line through the long summer days. We settled for the Moosomin Motel because it was the last room in town, it was after eight o'clock, and I was see-ing spots instead of the road in front of me.

Once I saw the room, I was tempted to chance the spots. But one look at the boys and I ignored the faded red-and-black-flocked wallpaper, the stained green toi-let and bathtub, the mismatched bedspreads on the sagging beds, and dumped my bags on the floor. The smell of disinfectant and mold was harder to ignore, but I knew I'd get used to it after a few minutes.

"Dibs on the bathroom."

Eric looked up from fiddling with the TV and said as if it were unthinkable, "There's no remote," his voice rising with despair. "No cable, either."

Mickey sat on the bed farthest from the door, his arms around Dexter, face buried in the dog's neck. He sagged almost as much as the beds.

"How about a before-bed snack?" Anything to cheer them up. Besides, we'd eaten lousy burgers almost four hours ago and if I was hungry, the boys would be starv-ing. "I saw a Kentucky Fried down the road. Chicken and fries? Maybe a little coleslaw?"

Mickey brightened slightly. "Wings, okay? That's all I want."

"Eric?"

He turned from the TV in disgust, leaving it half-tuned to a snow-flaked version of the news. "Yeah, okay, wings for me too. And fries. Extra ketchup."

As if I didn't know that Eric's favorite food was anything drowned in ketchup. I grabbed my purse and headed back out to the car. It felt odd when I got in to run down the street. I was alone in the car, alone in my aluminum shell. And that hadn't happened for so long I'd forgotten what it felt like.

I drove toward the red-and-white logo, my eyes locked onto it as if it were an oasis after weeks in the desert. I deliberately blanked my mind because I knew what the dark half of me was saying and I didn't want to hear it.

Didn't matter, though, blanked or not, the message got through to my body loud and clear. I drove right past the KFC, right through the town (which took all of three minutes), and out into the blackness of the prairie night.

I pulled over just outside of town, where the streetlights stopped and the true night began. I rolled down all the windows, undid my seat belt and took off, heading south, I thought. I laughed because it didn't matter which way I went, I was alone. *All by myself. Solitary.* And it was going to stay that way for as long as I kept driving.

I savored the silence, the sensation of space expanding around me. My foot lay heavy on the accelerator, my fingertips light on the steering wheel. The night seeped into the car, slowly, slowly, until I no longer consciously heard it. The rush of wind through the windows, the faint song of the cicadas, the lonesome howl of a train whistle, all vanished into the black hole of the night. I existed, in some strange and impossible way, in a vacuum.

I knew there were things I should remember, things I was supposed to be caring for, but I traveled in a dream. Nothing mattered outside the car. I couldn't control the shape of the dream and I didn't want to.

I drove, passing lighted farmhouses, a few cars, a couple of crossroads, some route signs that I ignored. I saw them all, but they were separate from me, from my experience and life inside the shell. They registered only as the weakest of blips on my radar. Alien and unknowable, unnecessary.

The few interruptions faded away until I found myself completely alone, surrounded by the blackest of nights, no sign of civilization, or even life. The song of the cicadas was gone. No farmhouses lit their candles to the darkness. No signs told me where I was.

I slowed down, pulled off the pavement onto the shoulder, the sound of the gravel against the tires grating to my ears. With the car and the lights turned off, the transformation was complete. Black as the bottom of a well, silent as that moment in the bathtub when you first discover that the sound of water in your ears is the sound of your own heart beating. The air on my face when I stepped out onto the road and leaned against the car pressed like a freshly washed flannel sheet, warm and soft and clean.

The night swirled around me. I closed my eyes,

shocked by the stars overhead, shocked by the way they reached down to the horizon. A faint red glow lined my eyelids. I sank into it.

The red glow reflected off a pond, a small deep cold pool of water. Bottomless. Somehow I knew it was bottomless. I knelt at the edge of it, my feet and legs bare on the smooth damp rocks. I was waiting. And I was scared. But my body was rooted into the ground, stuck like Krazy Glue to the rocks.

I knew if I opened my eyes, if I could somehow open them, the pond and my fear would vanish. But my eyelids ignored my pleas. They stayed closed, keeping me locked into the red world.

My body trembled, cowering in the dark, waiting. The ground shook. Or was it me? I tried to turn my head away from the pond, to see what was coming from behind me.

But I knew what made the ground shake. I knew what I waited for. I didn't need to see it to know. And I knew, too, it would rise from the pond. All I didn't know was what shape it would take on this particular night.

My deepest fears, my anxiety, my panic. They took myriad forms, rising, crawling, leaping out of the water and appearing on the ground in front of me and I was helpless before them. I'd been having this dream for years. I knew I couldn't save myself, had known that all along. All I wanted now was to see it coming. But even that was denied me.

Without warning, she appeared. Miranda Jane Roman. I'd never seen her before, never even imagined that she might appear in this place. Her face reflected reality. Grim and old and lonely, the cheery grin metamorphosed into tragedy. The woman I would become.

As always, it was tears that unglued my eyelids and opened them to the prairie sky. Not a sound broke the silence; not a movement marred the stillness.

My constant craving for silence and solitude was finally and completely answered. And it felt...it felt wrong. Standing in the prairie night I knew, for the first time in years, that I was in the wrong place. I might not know what the right place was, but I knew this was wrong. All I had to do was make a U-turn and I'd be headed back. It was almost too simple. All the biggest revelations were.

So that's what I did. I'd only been gone an hour, although it felt in some ways like a lifetime. I turned the car around, careful to check for oncoming vehicles (there were none) and equally careful not to end up in a ditch. I assumed there were ditches, it was too dark to see them. The road led straight back to Moosomin, a good thing as I hadn't read any signs and the map was, as always, in Mickey's possession.

The KFC was open, the smell of chicken and fries and grease familiar and comforting. I waited without concern while the single boy behind the counter dipped the basket of fries into the bubbling grease, while he

separated handfuls of wings from the rest of the body
parts on the morguelike warming trays. I waited while
he placed the hot fries in paper holders, then into the
red-and-white cardboard boxes, carefully nestling them
next to the chicken. He hauled out a handful of
ketchup packets, then two more, then another, stopping only when I nodded.

The motel still stood, no police cars, no ambulances
or fire engines. My worry, what little there was of it,
wasn't about those external things. Fire, murder, rape,
kidnapping. My anxiety was about how I would deal with
the certainty I'd been given. For given it was, by some
force outside myself, reaching out of that black prairie
night to tell me where I needed to be. What would I do
with that knowledge? I hoped the question would eventually answer itself. I hoped it wouldn't take too long.

The TV showed a snow-free picture when I opened
the door. Eric was sprawled on his belly across one bed,
his chin resting on his hands, his eyes intent on the
screen. Mickey had filched the flat pillows and piled
them up behind him, reclining like a sultan on a silk-
covered divan, Dexter at his side. All three of them
looked up at the noise of the door then back at the
screen. They hadn't even missed me.

I placed the food on the rickety table under the window and started eating my share of the chicken. The
taste of the salty coating, the smell of warm, moist,

greasy chicken, the sounds of the TV, the two boys breathing, Dexter panting, felt right to me.

I didn't know—how could I?—that the revelation I'd had in the car would change my life. But it didn't matter, because I felt sleepy, relaxed, and content in the ugliest motel room in the prairies. I finished my chicken watching a rerun of *The X-Files*.

I waited until the show was over, knowing the boys wouldn't hear a word if I spoke during the action.

"I'm going out to phone your mum. I'll be back in a few minutes."

The phone booth stood in solitary splendor next to the highway. I stood outside and listened to the night. Trucks and TVs from the motel, the hum of air conditioners in the windows. Laundry first? We were only two days from Cranberry Portage. Maybe it could wait.

"Hey," I said to the sleepy voice at the other end of the phone. "Just called to check in."

"Hmm," Susan said. "How're the boys?"

"They're fine. I'm fine. We should be there in a couple of days."

"That's good."

I heard her suppress a yawn.

"Go back to sleep. I'll call you earlier tomorrow night. We're running behind schedule today."

I would tell her I got lost, that I drove away from her boys, but not tonight. Not until we were home safe and sound and she could see that they were okay. Besides, I wanted to be sure my transformation would stick.

I felt sleep dropping onto me like a net I didn't want to escape. Soft and light as a spider's web, sleep gathered me up in its strong arms, wrapped me in them, cradling me to its chest. I might have been slipped a tranquilizer, or given an anesthetic. The need for sleep was so overwhelming I barely made it back to the room.

The lights were out, the TV flickering quietly in the corner, as I slipped under the covers. I didn't feel my head touch the pillow. I was asleep before it did.

Eric's Notebook

Randy disappeared last night. I didn't say anything to Mickey. He would have worried. I was hoping she wouldn't come back 'cause then I'd phone Mum and we could go home. Three hours, that's how long I was going to wait.

But she showed up just in time. She was smiling. A real smile, not the fake one she's been using. What does that mean?

One thing for sure. It means we're still going to Cranberry Portage. In a hurry. No stopping. Not that there's anywhere to stop. That's okay by me. The sooner we get there, the sooner we can turn around and go home.

I've been painting a little. I like the look of the prairies. It's simple. Flat. Uncrowded. So I can paint the small changes.

When I paint at home, I have to take things out, and I can never figure out what to leave. I have to get rid of trees and mountains. Here I put things in. Shades of color, small shapes, one tree. I like it.

CHAPTER 15

Earthworms, though in appearance a small and despicable link in the chain of nature, yet, if lost, would make a lamentable chasm.
—Gilbert H. White

Tom finished the house a few days before the reunion, although he thought it might be more accurate to say that Rosa Munde practically finished him in the process. He'd been working flat out for months and he was exhausted. Too tired to complete the outside, too broke to hire someone to choose furniture, he settled for one king-size bed for his room, three queen-size beds for the guest rooms, and matching quilts for each. One half hour at the Sears catalogue store and five thousand dollars later, Rosa Munde Guest House was open for business.

"Put me at the bottom of the list." He heard the plea in his voice as he reported his progress to Maude. "I'm not ready." He spread open his hands and enumerated the defects. "It'll be more like camping than a hotel. No furniture except beds and lawn chairs. The outside's still not painted. No rugs, no TV, tools and wood all over the place."

Maude smiled at him reassuringly. "We have rooms for everybody who said they were coming and a bunch left over for extras. I don't think we'll need you, but just in case, okay?"

Tom walked away, heading for the Coffee Shop, still anxious. He didn't trust Maude when she wore that smile. It meant she had some plan up her sleeve. He knew someone, some poor soul without a place to stay, would show up on Rosa Munde's porch, heralded by an apologetic phone call from Maude.

He had almost a week before the reunion. It was the most beautiful summer he could remember and he'd spent almost all of it—except the one day a week he'd given over to fighting the weeds and debris in the yard—inside the house.

He still loved her, but over the past grueling months he'd gotten to know her, inside and out, and now his love was tempered with a healthy dose of reality. Instead of a young and charming Sleeping Beauty waiting to be awakened by his kiss, Rosa Munde was an aging dowager aunt, sharp, cranky and opinionated. She knew what she wanted and she made damn sure he knew it too. Otherwise, floors started to buckle, windows and doors slammed, or swelled so they wouldn't shut, tools and supplies disappeared, only to appear in another part of the house days later. After he'd replaced them.

The old house had a mind of her own. Tom respected her for that. He'd come to think of Rosa Munde, Mona Charles and Maude Fowler as the ruling triumvirate, the three graces, of Cranberry Portage, at least of his part of it. They subtly, and not so subtly, arranged his life for him. Mona and Maude continually set him up with eligible women. Eligible in their eyes meant female, over eighteen and under sixty. Even single was a flexible concept. Separated for longer than a day, husband or boyfriend working up north on the pipeline, almost any woman was fair game. The first time Maude tried to set him up with a not-so-married woman, Tom was shocked. But he soon got used to it.

He politely and firmly said no to all of them. Still reeling from the shock of first love, he knew he wasn't ready for another relationship. He was barely able to handle the one he had.

He sat at his kitchen table six days before the reunion, planning his escape. Winnipeg. He'd pick up his canoes, the rest of his furniture (Maude and Rosa Munde would like that), have a few drinks with the people from the office, maybe even spend a day on the water on the way back up. He nodded at the fridge. That's exactly what he was going to do.

* * *

The trip to Winnipeg scared him. Instead of stepping back into the city as if he'd never left, he wandered its streets feeling lost, battered by the noise and dirt and the sheer weight of concrete. Instead of enjoying the companionship he thought he'd been missing, he didn't even pick up the phone. He hunkered down in his motel until the U-Store-It opened, then rushed across the city to pick up his stuff. He rented a trailer to get it home in one load. He wasn't coming back.

Two days too long and he drove out of the city. The only thing he was willing to say about Winnipeg was that it didn't take long to leave it.

Tom followed the old bus route out of the city, every turn and hump known to him.

It felt good to be alone. The trouble with Cranberry Portage, with Rosa Munde and Mona and Maude, was they were always there. Tom grinned again. Of course that would change. He'd never again spend months locked to the old house, or spend his spare time in town because he had neither time nor energy to do anything else.

The road north beckoned and all thoughts of Winnipeg disappeared. This was his life, this sun, the pungent romantic scent of grass dying in the heat of the prairie summer. The song of cicadas, the jet contrails giving shape and definition to the palest of blue skies. He raised his head to see the horizon. It settled around him, the earth and sky melting into one, a life encompassed in one look, a life stretching as far as he could see yet contained, understandable. He held it in his hands.

Tom had forgotten how it felt to do nothing, to enjoy the feel of the sun and the breeze on his body. But the hard work was mostly over. He needed to paint the outside of the house before the winter. Everything else could wait. The weather would hold at least through September—almost two months. He felt as if he were back in school contemplating summer vacation, only now the world spun faster and those two months would be gone before he knew it.

He had three days to put everything in order. Canoe, pack, house. As soon as the reunion was over he would get in his canoe and follow the water—get to know his new territory. He smiled as he drove. Three days. He'd better get a move on.

CHAPTER 16

If you attach a net to your car, you may collect insects that fly over roads. As dragonflies like open spaces, this should be a good method for collecting them.
—*The Sunshine Coast News*, September 14, 2005

Eric's Notebook

It's all different. And it happened so fast. I can't get my head around it. Randy's in a terrible hurry. We drive all day, hours and hours and hours of perfectly straight roads. We stop for food but that's it. She even ignores Mickey's pleas about this museum or that provincial park. And that's the weirdest thing of all.

Because before she left us that night, she did whatever Mickey said. I don't get it.

I don't care. The sooner we get there—to

that stupid Cranberry Portage—who would name their town that?—the sooner we can turn around and go home. So I hope she keeps it up. I figure we can get there, do whatever it is we're supposed to do, and get home in a week.

I need to go home. I want my own room, my stuff, my own bathroom.

And I want to see Mum. She sounds okay. Really okay. But I don't know. I think I sound okay when I talk to her, but I'm not. Neither's Mickey. He talks in his sleep.

And he keeps collecting more of those stupid dead bugs off the windshield. There's boxes of jars in the back seat, full of wings. And yellow sticky stuff in plastic envelopes. It's gross.

And he's always reading from those damn bug books. And mostly it's that old one. It's stuck in my head. Why would he read a book that's so old? And it's all wrong. Even I know that. The guy doesn't know anything about bugs. He's an idiot.

We'll be in Cranberry Portage tomorrow night and everything will change. While we drove late into the night, the sky above us turned black, lit almost as clearly as day by the brightest and steadiest of stars. And then one flashed across the sky and I remembered, just in time, just before it disappeared, to make a wish.

I wished Eric would talk, Dexter would behave, Mickey would stop worrying about the dragonflies on the windshield. And me? I didn't know. But I wished for change. Somehow.

The prairie skies seemed to spawn bugs, throwing them against the car as if they had appeared out of the clear blue skies. Mickey didn't care about any of them except the silver-winged dragonflies. He was obsessed with them, with their deaths against the windshield, as if it were somehow our fault, for being on the road at the wrong time, as if the air displaced by our passage lured them into an act they would otherwise have been able to avoid. Mickey believed it to be our fault.

And that belief was why, three or four or five times a day, he took my eyebrow tweezers—which would never again be used for their intended purpose—and carefully, almost lovingly, pried the wings from the splotches on the windshield. Placed them in jars and the jars into their boxes. We'd bought case after case of canning jars and Mickey used the labels to mark the occasion of the dragonflies' passing. Incongruous, really, to see "July, 9:25 a.m., outside Red Deer" instead of raspberry or strawberry or peach on those lovely oval labels embossed with colored fruit.

Odd, too, to look into the jars, past the raised designs and gold-colored lids, and see wings. Sometimes only one, sometimes half a dozen.

The boxes piled up, fitted precisely on the floor behind my seat. I didn't know what he planned to do with them; he didn't say. And the boxes were filling up faster as we progressed across the flat landscape. We bought the first box in a small town outside Hope on the Similkameen River and it lasted a week, the second we bought in Red Deer, five days later, the third, fourth and fifth in rapid succession after we could no longer see the mountains.

There were more bugs in the prairies. Of all kinds, although of course I knew only about the dragonflies. I couldn't help it. Once Mickey focused on something, he thought of nothing else. Over the years I'd learned everything about dinosaurs, about miniature submarines, about eagles and salmon and poisonous snakes. Not to mention Bruce Lee.

Mickey's room was a palimpsest of his enthusiasms, layer upon layer. He never got rid of the last thing, just buried it beneath the new one. Even Susan had given up cleaning anything other than the top layer.

So what did I know about dragonflies? They were big—some of them as big as small birds. They flew very quickly, and they could even fly backwards. So could salmon. Swim backwards, I mean. Dragonflies were mythological creatures, as old as dinosaurs. They had lots of nicknames: Devil's Darning Needle, Snake Doctor, Mosquito Hawk. I knew other things as well. Like exactly what a dragonfly looked like when squished against a windshield traveling one hundred kilometers an hour. And how long it took for the wings to turn into tattered flags of flashing light in the corner of my eye.

But it gave Mickey something to do; the dragonflies and Dexter kept him occupied. Eric didn't do anything except scribble in his notebook and listen to the same music over and over and over again. I watched his lips move as he mouthed the lyrics although I never heard a sound coming from him. It was as if he'd determined silence was the only way he could make it through. I said a silent thank-you that the boys were so different, that Eric's silence could be balanced by Mickey's chatter.

But the last few days had brought unwanted insights. I came to realize that despite the external differences of how we coped, what was happening to the three of us inside was more alike than not. We were all scared. We were homesick. We needed to see Susan. Her cheerful voice and reassurances weren't enough, not nearly enough, to dispel the picture we retained of her.

She lay in the hospital bed covered with a pale blue blanket. Gray and pasty, her face practically vanished into the pillow. Her hair was lank, her arms and hands covered with bruises, big, ugly, painful-looking ones. And then there were the tubes, attached to her arms with tape, running out from under the covers, connecting to places I didn't want to imagine.

She looked sick. But she also looked wrong. Shrunken, of course. But I could hardly bear to look at her, to see how her shape had changed, how she had changed. How she was experiencing the sickness I'd spent years imagining.

And then she smiled and sent us away, told us to enjoy ourselves, that she would be okay and much happier to be thinking about us, her loved ones, relaxed and having a fun vacation. And I pretended to believe her. I guessed the boys did, too. Because none of us had questioned her decree, we simply went home and started packing.

The three of us became conspirators, locked into our own inability to talk about the thing, the dreaded thing that underlay every single moment of our days and nights. Because if we once said it, once acknowledged the monster, it would become real. Susan would die.

But not talking about it, while making it possible to get through the days, also meant that the three of us walked around with big black holes in our stomachs. And those holes never went away. For me, that hole was an amplifier. The anxiety I'd learned to co-exist with over the years blossomed into panic. I had no idea what it meant for Eric and Mickey.

We couldn't go on like this and I spent hours, days, nights trying to come up with a solution. The trouble, of course, was it had to be a solution I had the courage to instigate.

And that let out a lot of my ideas. I was pretty sure, no I was absolutely certain, that I couldn't come right out and say it. Even thinking about saying it made me nauseous. But in the end it felt like the only choice.

So here I was in yet another prairie Laundromat, the heat rising from the dryers in practically visible waves. The sweat poured down my back, my forehead, my thighs and my neck, then dried when I stepped outside for a breath of air, turning my hair into chicken peaks.

My mother sat on a dryer, vibrating slightly. She loved the heat, couldn't get enough of it. She never perspired. Never cried either, or peed that I could remember. Even at the end, in the hospital, I never saw her eyes water or the bag for her catheter fill. I wondered, sometimes, if she'd been dehydrated as a child, all the moisture squeezed out of her.

I stood next to the phone, contemplating my fingers. Biting the cuticles, picking at the dry skin. Carefully, though, because I knew it wouldn't take much to send me over the edge, to dissipate the tiny particles of courage I'd gathered around myself. If I bit down too far, pulled too hard, the swelling of blood would be enough. I'd take it as a sign. It would be a sign. I was making a mistake. So I was careful. A little bite here, a little tug there, and at the slightest hint of pain I went on to the next finger.

My conversation with Susan when I finally dialed her number was no different than usual.

"You're almost there. Are you excited? I bet the boys are. Mickey sounded over the top this morning."

Didn't she know those boys anymore? How could she think they might be excited about Cranberry Portage and seeing people and places they didn't know? And without her?

"Are you sure you can't come? Just for a couple of days? We could pick you up at the airport on the way by."

We'd been having the same discussion for days. It had come to me in the heart of the prairies that this was the best answer. We'd all see Susan, she'd be fine, we'd be reassured and I wouldn't have to do anything at all.

"Randy."

I knew that tone of voice. I knew the answer, too. "I know, I know, but we all want to see you. And you need to meet Dexter."

"I can't come. I can't get on an airplane with the treatments. It's all the potential germs and stuff while my immune system is already compromised." She explained it to me, again, as if I were a child.

I wanted to yell, *It's Steve, it's because you love him more than us,* even though I knew that wasn't true, but I wanted her to be at fault. I wanted to blame her. Because I knew if she didn't come—*when* she didn't come—I was going to have to talk to the boys.

"I had my checkup this morning."

"What did they say?"

"I'm doing fine, much better than they expected. They're cutting back on the post-op treatments. Looks like I'll be done before you get back."

"And?"

"I've got as good a chance as anybody. That's all they can say. But Steve says…"

I heard the smile in her voice when she said his name and grimaced at the bolt of envy racing through me.

"Steve says?"

"That I'll be fine. That he didn't wait this long to meet the perfect woman to give her up now."

"He's right," I said. "You are perfect. I'm glad he recognizes that."

"How are my boys?"

This was always her last question, the indication she was tiring. Time to wind it up.

"They're fine. Missing you, of course, but we're all looking forward to getting there tomorrow and getting out of this damn car. Why didn't I rent a minivan?"

Susan laughed as I intended. Good night. Good night. Talk to you tomorrow. And I was left to my own resources. Damn. Damn. Damn. I couldn't leave it any longer. Things, the boys, our lives, Dexter, everything was getting out of hand. And I knew the reason. Which meant I had to deal with it.

I sat down in the chair, red this time, the sweat

making my body cling to the nubbled surface. I ignored it.

It's never as bad as your imagination makes it out to be.

I looked around. I'd never seen another person in all these prairie Laundromats and here was someone, right in the very last one. But there wasn't. And there was nowhere to hide, either.

It's the anticipation that kills you, like going to the dentist. It never hurts as much as you expect.

"Mum?"

"Who else?"

The tub on the dryer vibrated though the laundry was still in the washing machine. Why hadn't I noticed that before? But I had, and put it down to trucks passing on the highway.

That's why I didn't plan things, or think about them ahead of time. What's the point? A creature of impulse, that's what I was.

Yeah, right up to the very end. She never gave a single thought to consequences.

Why should I?

Great, now she was reading my mind.

What else can I do? I don't have ears, or eyes for that matter. Besides, you've never been one for speaking your mind. The only way to tell what you really meant was to read your mind. Though I must say I thought I'd lost my touch that summer you turned twelve. Guess not.

I walked out the door and sat on the curb. This was too much. Maybe I thought I wanted her to talk to me but I didn't, not really.

Is it cooler out there? You never did much like the heat. Inherited your dad's fair skin. He never tanned, just burned, over and over again. Now Susan, she's like me. Skin like an Indian.

She was going to keep talking and there was no way for me to stop her. I saw that now. So I settled back on the curb and waited for her to have her say.

I am talking because you need somebody to tell you what to do. You need help.

"No. I don't need help, especially yours. I didn't need it when you were alive, I don't need it now."

Then why are you stewing like this? Not sleeping. Running away from your responsibilities. Oh, yes, I know exactly what you did.

"Okay. Okay. Have your say. Tell me what I need to do and then go away."

Oh, Randy, Randy, Randy. You're such a mess.

"Whose fault is that?"

You want me to tell you it's mine? Well, I won't. Because it's nobody's fault. It's just the way it is.

"You didn't love me."

There. It was said. The thing that had ruined my life was out in the open.

I loved you, still love you, but your ways and mine were different. You didn't recognize it for love. But it was.

"Not like you loved Susan."

The second thing.

Susan is like your dad. I fretted about you because you reminded me of me. And I knew what kind of trouble that meant. It's harder to love yourself.

I pondered that. She was right. But that didn't mean I was ready to forgive her.

You don't have to forgive me, just yourself. And you have to do right by my grandsons.

And as quickly as that, the connection was severed, as if the phone lines had been cut, leaving dead air. I knew she was gone for good. And I knew she was right. At least about the boys.

Somehow I had to talk to them about Susan, had to find the courage to tell them of my fears so that they could express theirs. Why me, though? Why did I, who'd never been able to expose myself, have to be the one to do this?

I sat in the Laundromat and practiced my speech, building line upon line, polishing them until they shone, even though I knew I would never get to speak them. Having them ready, having them perfect, was the only way I could imagine doing this. Because how could I have this conversation without a script?

The black started to fade out of the night as I folded the final T-shirt and made my way back to the motel. I opened the door and checked their breathing but I didn't go in. Instead, I closed the door behind me and sat down in the white plastic chair in front of the window and watched the sun come up.

CHAPTER 17

Two different insects—one large and one small, one delicate and one tough—should not be put in the same collecting bottle. They may damage one another.
—*The Sunshine Coast News*, September 14, 2005

Of course the sun rose, of course the motel woke up around me. I watched until the whole row of suites—all fourteen of them—emptied out. And it was still only eight o'clock. The chambermaids started rattling their carts at the far end of the row, moving fast, racing through the rooms. When they blocked my sun, I stood up and waited in front of our door, arms crossed over my breasts.

"Shh," I said. "My nephews are still sleeping. We had a tough day yesterday."

They smiled and nodded and tiptoed their carts around me to work on the room next to ours.

I opened our door and whistled quietly. Dexter needed to go out. He cocked one eye, spotted me and closed it again. His beloved boys were safe and he, like them, enjoyed a lie-in. I'd let them sleep this morning until they woke on their own, even if it meant paying for an extra day when we, inevitably, went past the official checkout time. What difference did another twenty bucks make?

The coffee shop beckoned me. From the booth in the front window, there was a clear line of sight to the door of our room, so I felt safe sitting there, looking at the pictures in the newspaper, reading nothing, not even the captions. I was too tired. Almost fourteen hours on the road yesterday and no sleep at all last night. I should be used to it, but I figured out you never got used to sleeplessness. What happened was you developed a kind of torpor, a way of getting through the day with the least possible exertion.

And that wasn't the best condition to be in when planning my first serious conversation with my nephews. I sat in that booth, the sun heating the red vinyl bench until it stuck to my legs and back, until it felt like the vinyl melted beneath me like a chocolate bar in the sun. I lifted my legs and checked the backs to make sure they weren't coated with red. Pulling them from the vinyl hurt, but no red remained once I unstuck them.

"Eric. Mickey." I practiced in a tiny whisper, keeping my lips together to avoid stares from the waitress behind the counter. She'd pursed her lips when I only ordered coffee, when I insisted on a booth, each time she refilled my cup.

"Boys." Still not the carefree, relaxed tone I needed.

"Guys." Now that was it, the perfect tone. Not too serious, all inclusive, they wouldn't suspect a thing.

"Guys…"

But what came next? I wanted to tell them I was scared too, that I understood what they were going through because I lost my mother the same way. But I was a grown-up when it happened. And Susan wasn't dying. That's what she said, what the doctors said, what Steve said, and though I had my doubts, I didn't want Eric and Mickey to hear them.

"Guys," I started again. "I talked to your mum last night. They're cutting back on her treatments because she's doing so well."

Could I say that without them hearing the question I asked myself? Were they cutting back because the treatments were hopeless? Could I say it so they'd believe me?

The six cups of coffee made me shake. I needed to eat but couldn't bear the thought of bacon and eggs. And it was too hot for oatmeal. But that was what I wanted. Oatmeal with condensed milk and a layer of brown sugar just like my father made every Sunday morning until the day he left us.

Another memory resurfaced like a dead fish floating

in a tank. It wasn't as surprising this time now that I knew they were there somewhere. All I had to do was to wait for something to trigger them. Thinking about John Wayne. Seeing oatmeal on the menu.

Maybe that day was the day my life had changed. It was cool enough to see my breath when I got out of bed that morning, cool enough for Dad to make oatmeal before I went off to Sunday School. Just the two of us were up. Mum always slept in on Sundays; she said she was entitled to one break a week. And Susan wasn't feeling well, so it was the two of us, just the way I liked it. He didn't disappear until later in the week while I was at school. That breakfast was the last thing I remembered.

He was standing at the stove when I came down the stairs, unshaven, his hair sticking up in spikes, his T-shirt untucked, his feet bare on the cold linoleum.

"It's almost ready, sunshine. Just grab the brown sugar, will you?"

We talked about…what? I wanted to invest that conversation with meaning, to make it full of insight and love and enough advice to last a lifetime, but my memory stopped right there, reaching for the brown sugar. I tried to remember something else, anything else, but I couldn't.

I wanted to remember more. Now that I'd started—now that I had those two small memories—I wanted them all. Birthday parties, trips in the car, eating ice cream, helping in the yard. I even wanted the spankings and the angry words when I'd been bad. I wanted to fill in those blank pages from my childhood. I wanted my father back.

Maybe the house we'd lived in would be my Ouija board, tarot cards, channeler, the tool I needed to rediscover the first six years of my life. When I sat in that kitchen again, I believed my father would appear. Memories would wash over me so quickly I would have to fight against drowning in them. But I wouldn't drown. I'd revel, wallow like a pig in a mudhole.

The urgency to be on the road struck me full force. Time the boys were up. We'd already wasted—I looked up at the clock—a half day of driving. No way we'd get to Cranberry Portage tonight, so I'd have another night before I had to talk to the boys. Before we reached journey's end, that was my promise. And I'd keep it. But I didn't have to do it today. The sun shone, they'd had plenty of sleep. Maybe it would be a good day.

Nope. It wasn't. Mickey woke up with an earache, Eric with the sulks, Dexter with diarrhea from last night's chocolate milkshakes. Perfect. It was the worst day yet on the road trip from hell. Mickey moaned in the back seat, we stopped every half hour to let Dexter out, and Eric exuded a black cloud of unhappiness so thick I couldn't see his features through it.

I settled into the misery as if I belonged there. In some odd way it felt comfortable and familiar to me.

The days spent on the road, those long, cranky days and endless sleepless nights, had more than prepared me for this day.

The landscape rushed past us, the world outside the car moving instead of us. I remembered old black-and-white movies. There was always a scene with a couple sitting in a car or the back seat of a taxi while the camera focused on the landscape driving past. Because it was perfectly obvious that the car was standing still and the landscape was moving. That's the way I felt today.

It made me feel off-kilter, the way I'd felt before we left Vancouver, when the boys were still in school and I was at home all day. I'd never been off work except to go on vacation so the city—the daytime workday city— felt as odd to me as if I were seeing it through tinted glasses. The rhythms were wrong. I was in the wrong place at the wrong time. I'd worked Monday to Friday, nine to five, for over twenty years.

Who in the hell were all those people walking the city streets? Didn't they have to work? The tourists were easily recognizable, their backpacks and lost looks and obviously sore feet giving them away. But everyone else? They couldn't all be restaurant workers. It was the weirdest sensation, like Alice going through to Looking Glass world. It made me dizzy.

That's how the landscape racing past made me feel. Our aluminum shell sealed itself around us, shutting out all the noise and light and air from the world passing by. We were in a deep-sea-diving bell, watching the water get darker and deeper and colder as we got winched down from the ship on the surface.

I hoped the man himself, Jacques Cousteau, the hero of my childhood, watched over us, because there was no other way I could see for us to be safe. The car, the trip, everything had been ripped out of my control. I kept my hands on the steering wheel, my eyes on the road, my foot on the gas pedal, but I knew it was useless. It wouldn't make any difference if I let go. I wasn't in control. Of anything. I never had been.

Oh shit. Another revelation. My perfect life—job, house, no kids or husband—was a house of straw waiting for the big bad wolf to come along and huff and puff and blow it down. Sure he'd have to step back and take deep breaths, maybe rub his palms together. Sure he'd have a red face and a sore throat at the end of it.

But when I thought about the big picture, it hadn't taken much to pull down my house. Because all the things that had happened in the past couple of months—Susan getting sick, losing my job, traveling with two messed-up boys and an untrained puppy— were only catalysts. The real thing, the trigger for everything, was memory. Such a small thing, really.

A few synapses sparking in my brain, making connections, getting to know one another, giving up the family feud and talking. Brain cells meeting for the first time, shaking hands. That's all it took for me to see what a sham my perfect life had turned out to be. Control. It was all about control.

Because I'd lost control of my life when I lost my father, not only physically, but psychically as well. I had lost the sight and smell and touch and those things were important. But the memories counted. They were what I needed, what I couldn't do without, what I'd spent my life trying to replace. By living so it could never happen again.

I closed my eyes to think about all this. The car faltered, shifting without warning and suddenly, our aluminum shell moved across a completely still landscape, as if we traveled across a photograph or a painting. No motion, not even a hint of a breeze or the zip of birds' wings. No dragonflies on the windshield. Only the car and the four of us moving across the surface of the earth.

Mickey screamed. I looked up to see the highway sign heading straight for our front bumper, the gravel spinning beneath the tires, Eric desperately trying to wrench control from my hands, which were locked onto the wheel.

The brakes squealed as I pumped them, twisting into the direction of the skid. Eric kept his hands on mine, a warning not to lose it again. A cloud of dust hid the road behind us as we pulled to a stop.

"Everyone okay?"

The car filled with silence.

"I'm fine, Eric." I pried his fingers from the wheel. "Really."

The shutters slammed down over his face. He nodded and settled back into his seat though his discomfort at doing so was obvious.

"I've got us this far, haven't I?"

No answer from anyone. Well, I had got us this far and I'd be fine. I would be. Somehow we'd all be fine. The tires spun as I headed off the gravel and back onto the highway, careful to keep my eyes open and on the road.

"Wait," I whispered to my memories. "Wait."

Eric's Notebook

Now what do I do? First she runs away, now she's driving like a lunatic. She's lost it. But I can't tell Mum. I can't. It's getting worse, everything is getting worse. I have to be strong for Mickey. That's what Mum said: *Look after him, okay?* But she didn't know what would happen, did she? Does that mean I can tell her?

What if we end up in a ditch or a lake? She'll be sorry she sent us away then. When she hears it on the news, *Tourists drown in lake after car leaves highway, driver asleep at the wheel.* I can see the car sinking to the bottom, me pounding on the windows, Mickey screaming. What a lousy way to go. But it might happen. It probably will happen. Is that enough? Can I tell her?

I'm scared. I can't tell her that. I can't tell anyone. I hate being here. There's no one to talk to except Mickey and he's always talking about bugs. Yuck. I want to talk about...

What? What do I want to say? I want to tell Mum to let us come home. I want to tell Mickey everything's okay. I want to tell Randy to straighten up. And I can't say anything.

Fuck, fuck everything. I wish I could close my eyes and when I woke up this trip would be over. That's what I want.

CHAPTER 18

Do not carry acetone or cyanide in your pockets
and use plastic containers instead of glass. A glass
container combined with a fall could inject you
with the poison you are carrying.
—*The Sunshine Coast News*, September 14, 2005

The blue disappeared from the sky for the first time in
weeks, leeched out until only a sullen sheet of col-
orlessness remained. August, yet the sky looked like winter. I shivered, though whether from the quickly chilling
air or the sight of the sky ahead of us, I didn't know.

I'd never seen anything like the sky overhead. Even
the winter storms on the Coast couldn't match it.
Those skies were filled with movement, black clouds
hurling themselves across the expanse, chased by rain
and roaring winds. Coastal storms were exciting, full of
color and motion. This sky settled down over the earth
like a pillow, smothering everything it touched.

I reached for Eric's shoulder and pointed out the

window. He grudgingly turned his head, stared, fascinated, for a few minutes before pulling the earphones from his head.

"Look, Mick. It's weird."

"Yeah," I said, "like something's waiting to happen."

Like Dorothy's tornado in *The Wizard of Oz*, and like Dorothy, I had no idea what might happen. I was more nervous than usual because we drove in isolation. No cars, power lines, not a house for miles. The last signpost—Mickey, as always, read it out loud—said *Check your gas. Last services for 221 kilometers*. I had no idea how many of those kilometers we'd yet to travel, but we were right smack in the middle of the emptiness.

"Should we pull over?"

"Don't know." Eric looked out at the sky with a dazed expression on his face. I expected it mirrored my own.

Mickey hugged Dexter. "No," he said, "keep going."

"You're right. There'll be a town soon. Besides, nothing's happening."

What I meant was that nothing was happening compared to the Coast. But I felt the air pressure changing just as if we were going up in a hurry, in a plane.

"Yawn," I said, and handed out the leftover mints from last night's dinner. "It'll make your ears pop."

I didn't know what to do for Dexter whining in the back seat, but Mickey did. He gave him the bubble gum he'd removed to suck on the mint I handed him.

And Dexter didn't swallow it in one gulp as he did anything else even faintly resembling food; he chewed it like he would a bone.

The only sounds were the wet chompings of Dexter and the occasional sucking sound from the boys or me. I rolled down the window, hoping to equalize the air pressure and give my sinuses a break. Instead, a perceptible chill entered the car. I thought of dozens of movies, of *X-Files* episodes where the air cooled rapidly in a single location. It meant a ghost. Always.

I knew if there were to be ghosts, this would be exactly the kind of place they'd appear. And I knew, of course I knew there were no ghosts on this deserted stretch of highway. But knowing that didn't lessen my rising tension. If anything, it heightened. I knew what to do about ghosts. Try to communicate with them. They only found the energy to manifest themselves if they had something to say. Talking to a ghost would be easy compared to the frightening world surrounding us now.

Because I didn't recognize it, because I had nothing to compare it to, I didn't know what to do. Pull over? Under a tree or not? Keep going? Fast or slow? Turn back? Try and outrun whatever it was? Stay in the car or get out?

In the end, as always, I settled for the path of least resistance. I kept going, driving just under the posted limit, my hands clenched on the steering wheel, and watched, as did the boys, all of us waiting for whatever was going to happen. We watched the unsettling sky. We scanned the road ahead, the scattered paths leading off it, hoping for something to appear that might provide shelter, safety, another opinion. A gas station, an abandoned cottage, a town. And we waited for the world around to explode.

The sky darkened first with the subtlety of a movie theater just before the previews. One minute you're squinting at the magazine on your lap, the next it's pitch-black. And you couldn't remember the exact moment when you could no longer see the print on the page, when light turned into dark.

It happened without warning. The heavy sky, gray and featureless, became black, but not the black of night, but rather the black of…what? I didn't know. Maybe the black of fear, faintly lit from within, the light, what there was of it, cool and distant, not caring that it was being used only to prove the superiority of the dark. Because the dark was what we saw, a huge black pillow pressing closer and closer until it felt as if a cosmic hand lay heavy on top of it, leaning all of its weight on the pillow on top of the car, squeezing the air out of our lungs.

I couldn't drive, could barely breathe. I pulled over as far as I could get onto the shoulder. There was no shelter. We were trapped in the northern tundra. The few trees grew stunted and bent, no taller than the car. The four of us huddled in our makeshift shelter, the cooling engine ticking into the silence. I knew from their faces that the boys knew the aluminum shelter surrounding us might be insufficient to protect us.

"It's better than nothing," I said, mostly to break the increasingly ominous silence.

Eric reached up and pressed his hand against the roof, and we watched as first the interior padding, then the outer shell yielded to the pressure.

"Not much better," he said.

It dragged on forever—that wait in the car—but it couldn't have been more than a couple of minutes before it began. In some ways, the relief, the cessation of anticipation, knowing, finally, what it was, made the fear feel almost secondary. But maybe that was only true in retrospect because what happened next was the most frightening thing I'd ever seen.

The stillness grew deeper, heavier, darker, the whole world an unlit cave, not a single breath of air moved. Eric and I, without consultation, pulled the bags and boxes from the back seat into the front and shoehorned ourselves into the back, Mickey, with Dexter on his lap, in the middle. I clasped Eric's hands, one in front, one in back, forming a circle around the small shaking boy and the big trembling dog. And we waited.

A clap of thunder overhead set Dexter barking and

the three of us yelping. But all sound vanished into the roar of the wind, throwing itself against the car until I couldn't tell what or who shook. Pebbles and rocks and branches banged against the car, small, almost unfelt touches beside the wind and the thunder.

We curled around one another instinctively, our heads lowered over our knees. Yet none of us could resist quick, furtive looks at the astonishing world outside the car. We'd look for a moment at the swirling lumpy mass of air and dirt roaring past us then bury our heads until the storm pulled at us again. It contained both compulsion and repulsion, pushing us away, pulling us in, and not one of us strong enough to ignore it and keep our heads safely down.

A louder, heavier thump on the roof brought me out of my crouch. Another. Another. Thump, thump, crash. Something broke the windshield. Thump, crash. I pulled blankets from underneath us and draped them over our heads, tucking the ends underneath. The wind was in the car with us, tugging at the blanket, trying to rip it from our hands, trying to rip the hair from our heads, our teeth from our jaws.

Thump. Crash. The tinkle of glass breaking a sweet counterpart to the heavy roar of the intruding wind and the violence of the blows against the car.

And then, far more suddenly than it began, the storm was over. My ears popped, and sunlight shone through the blanket. I huddled in toward the boys and Dexter more closely, scared to look out, scared to remove my cover, my safety, and reveal the devastation.

It felt like those too many nights when I woke, fear clutching my heart and lungs and bowels, when I hid beneath the covers and tried desperately to forget the images that came to me in my restless sleep. The city shattered, trees ripped from the earth, sidewalks and bridges and streets crumpled and lying in patches of broken concrete. Holes in the midst of still green lawns, holes filled with dirty black water and holding who knew what within their murky depths.

But hours later, still sleepless, the images burned into my brain, onto my retinas, so when I removed the covers, the first things I saw in the light of dawn were ghost images of my nightmares, superimposed upon the perfect day beginning in the real world.

But Mickey and Eric hadn't learned my patience or my fear. They tugged the blankets from their heads and mine to reveal a fairytale world. It glittered under a brilliant blue sky, the stubby trees turned an obscenely bright green, washed clean and new by the storm. And the ground lay thickly covered with crystal, sparking fire into the sky.

No wind blew through the broken windshield, no thunder or lightning disturbed the peace. The warm air met the ice on the ground to create a faint mist, rising to my knees when I stepped out of the car and onto the snow. I leaned down to touch it. Not snow, but ice crystals the size of my hand, packed tightly on the ground as if they were Japanese oranges, the kind wrapped carefully in whisper-thin green paper and then stacked one by one into a wooden crate for their long journey across the ocean.

Dexter bounced out of the car and across the whiteness, chasing balls of ice thrown by the boys, for him, and at each other. The demarcation of the ice crystals was as clear and certain as a border on a map. For a hundred feet in front of us, the ground was white. Past the border, nothing had happened.

The roof of the car bore dents the size of my fist, the windshield shattered in half-a-dozen places. I touched the center of the web of cracks and the glass crumpled, falling away from my hand into the car. The square pellets were smooth and tidy, like miniature building blocks.

We couldn't go anywhere without a windshield. The bugs would blind me, or rocks, or another storm full of hailstones the size of oranges. Grapefruit. Baseballs. For the first time I wished I'd taken Susan's advice and bought a cell phone. But it probably wouldn't work in the wilderness so all we could do was wait for a car to pass us and take a message to the nearest garage. At least the boys were having fun, I heard them laugh though they'd disappeared into some gully not far from the car.

I brushed the fragments of glass from the front seat, put the seat back and settled in, the sun warming my face and arms. I fell asleep.

It might have been five minutes or an hour before I woke to see a huge red truck parked behind me. The boys, Dexter, and whoever drove the truck were nowhere to be seen. Panic raced through me, making my legs and eyelids twitch. Where were they? Who had got out of the truck? Why hadn't I heard them? I stumbled getting out of the car, fell to my knees on the pavement, steaming now in the sun. I looked down at my hands. Splinters of glass—the square pieces I hadn't believed sharp enough to cut—shone from my palms. And my knees, too, although I couldn't see that until I stood up.

Pain filled my body, radiating up to my head from the tiny blocks of glass shining from my skin. I ignored it, limping first, then running headlong in the direction where I'd last seen the boys. I yelled.

"Mickey. Eric. Where are you?"

I hoped to scare whoever was with them, frighten him into letting them go. I whistled for Dexter and heard his joyful bark in return with a surge of relief. No kidnapper, no molester, would allow Dexter to live.

"Eric. Mickey. Answer me."

I staggered down the gully, my legs weak beneath me. I fell, landing heavily, ramming the glass in further. I didn't care. I'd dragged them across the country, I'd almost lost Mickey once before, I'd deserted them. I couldn't let anything happen to them. Not now. Not ever.

"Eric." I yelled, though my voice seemed to attenuate, becoming too thin to hear the instant it left my mouth.

"Mickey. Mickey. Where are you?"

Tears ran down my face. I tasted the salt. It matched the blood on my palms, running down my calves from my knees. Salt. I was losing my last connection to the Coast, to my home, becoming less salty, shedding that which locked me to the edge of the land. Salt dripping from me one molecule at a time, in thick drops of blood and thin, light tricklings of tears.

I slid down to the bottom of the gully on my butt. I couldn't stand, it hurt too much. I squinted up into the sun.

"Randy?" Mickey's voice was shaking, frightened.

Another joined him. "Randy? Are you okay?" Eric, less frightened, but the shift in octaves still obvious. Worry, there, not fear. Not yet.

A third, deeper, more adult voice overrode the others. It sounded warm, friendly, and the competence in it unclenched my stomach.

"Randy?"

How did he know my name?

"Randy? I'm going to pick you up, okay? Take you back to the car."

I nodded. Good idea, I thought, just before I fainted.

Eric's Notebook

We met the best guy today. And we finally made it to Cranberry Portage. Randy's in the hospital getting her knees and hands fixed.

She fell onto the glass that fell out of the windshield. Tom, Tom Webb, took most of it out but some bits were too deep. So he drove us here and we took her to the hospital.

We're at a coffee shop. Waiting. Tom just phoned. Randy has to stay overnight. They gave her some kind of drugs. So we're going to stay with Tom. He phoned Mum and everything. So did I, before he came back. Just to check. They even let Dexter into the coffee shop though he has to sit on the floor and be quiet. Two old ladies are sitting in the next booth. Tom introduced them. I can't remember their names but they're okay, I guess. Don't say much, not to us. But I think they're watching us. Not creepy, just careful.

Mickey's talking to Mum. He promised he wouldn't say what happened. We both did. When we dropped Randy at the hospital, she told us not to say anything. But of course Mum knows 'cause Tom must have told her.

This isn't a very big place, not like home. Tom says Mum and Randy grew up in his house.

His house even has a name. Rose something, I think. Anyway, the ladies told us we should go to the opening ceremonies for the reunion. Sounds like the Olympics. I hope they have fireworks. I don't care, but Mickey loves them.

This trip is a mess. Now Randy's in the hospital overnight, but at least we have Tom. Mum said he was okay. She checked. But I'll keep my eyes open, even so. Because how can she tell just from talking to him on the phone? Maybe he's just trying to convince her to let us stay so he can... But I don't think so. I'll tell Mickey to lock his door just in case.

CHAPTER 19

Perseverance will accomplish anything…
—Gilbert H. White

Tom dropped the two boys and the dog at the Coffee Shop. He left Randy in the truck while he took Eric and Mickey inside, introduced them to Maude and Mona sitting in the next booth, and told them to order whatever they wanted.

"I shouldn't be too long. The hospital's just down the street. But I'll call you—" he nodded at the phone by the cash register "—when I know what's up."

Eric looked only slightly less shaken than his younger brother. He swallowed before he spoke.

"Thanks, Tom. She's going to be okay, isn't she?"

"Oh, sure. I've seen things like this before." A lie. Tom had never seen glass burrow so deep it moved underneath her pale skin like some alien creature searching for the center of her body.

"She'll be out today, right?"

That was Mickey and his voice trembled.

"Well…" Tom stroked his chin in what he thought to be a reassuring manner, a gesture he'd learned only since moving to Cranberry Portage. "I should think so. It was only a little glass. She'll be sore for a while—" an understatement if he ever heard one "—but she'll be fine. Perfectly fine."

He spent the first hour in the waiting room trying not to hear the muffled cries coming from behind the swinging door. He spent the next hour going over dozens of plans of what to do with the boys if Randy—Miranda Jane Roman, and what a coincidence this whole thing turned out to be—couldn't leave the hospital for a couple of days. He was interrupted by a nurse telling him that Randy was sleeping but he could pick her up in the morning.

"Did you want to see her?" the nurse said over her shoulder, walking away, confident he would follow.

And she was right. Tom wanted to see her. Wanted, for the boys' sake, to make sure she was okay. Wanted even more, for his own sake, to make sure her eyes were as beautiful as he remembered.

She reminded him of Rosa Munde as she'd been the first time he saw her. Damaged by neglect but her strength and beauty and bones were as obvious to him as were the bones of the land, his land, beneath the trappings of summer.

It was something Tom Webb had always done, something that came to him as a teenager when he began spending his time in the country. First he felt it, learning the skeleton, the strong granite spine of the Canadian Shield, buried deep beneath the earth and flora. As he grew more experienced, he began to see it, the evidence clear in the tiny hummocks of moss, the subtle changes of color when the rock thrust closer to the surface, the faint distant waves of the hills.

Now, he'd somehow learned to use that skill on things other than the land. On his house. On people. Miranda Jane Roman was as strong as granite although she seemed unaware of that strength. It was buried as deep as the Canadian Shield. He looked down at her, the bandages on her hands no whiter than her skin. She opened her eyes, compelled, he thought, by his gaze, but they were blank, dazed by the medication. He blinked and she slept again.

Time to solve his more immediate problem. He thrust Miranda to the back of his mind. The boys had to come first. Miranda had given her sister's number to the nurse as emergency contact when she checked in. He'd memorized it and dialed it now, standing in the waiting room.

"Susan? Susan McGivern?"

"Yes."

"I'm calling from Cranberry Portage."

"What's wrong? Who are you? My boys…"

He heard the panic in her voice and rushed on. "My name is Tom Webb. Eric and Mickey are fine. I picked them up on the highway, their windshield was shattered in a hailstorm so they couldn't drive."

"Randy. You haven't mentioned Randy." The woman's voice slowed with the onset of fear. "Oh, God. What happened?"

"She's okay. She got cut, her hands and her knees, by the glass. But they got it all out. She's sedated but she can leave the hospital tomorrow."

By the time he'd told her the whole story—and it was the *whole* story—from discovering Rosa Munde right up to his trip to Winnipeg, with many side trips into his past to make things perfectly clear (Susan was so easy to talk to that Tom found it almost impossible to shut up), they'd become fast friends. They'd exclaimed about the coincidence of Tom buying Susan's childhood home and then saving her sister on the highway, laughed about Dexter and made plans for the boys to stay with him.

She'd asked for references—he gave her Mona and Maude—and after she telephoned to check, he'd made a quick call to the Coffee Shop to reassure Eric and Mickey and a quick trip back to Miranda's room to reassure himself. And then he phoned Maude.

"My rooms are gone," he said. "The Romans are going to stay with me over the reunion."

Tom heard the satisfaction in her voice as if she'd planned it that way all along.

"Good. There's three of them and you have three rooms." He heard a pencil tick against her always present list.

"Perfect. I'll see you at the opening ceremonies tonight. And bring the boys. But not the dog. He's not trained yet. You can work on that this weekend."

He wondered, fleetingly, just how much she'd learned from Eric and Mickey, just what she knew that he didn't. Tom shrugged. What difference would it make? She was always going to know more than he did and there was nothing at all to be done about it. He checked on Randy one more time, bending to touch his lips to her forehead.

"Sleep well. I'll pick you up tomorrow."

This time, when her eyes fluttered open, panic clouded them.

"They're fine. Eric and Mickey and Dexter are fine."

The panic receded but waited there, behind her eyes, behind the medication, peering out like fox kits from their burrow, waiting for the next bad thing to happen, thinking of him as an eagle or a wolf or a bear. Thinking of him, of the world, as an enemy. But he was a savior.

"It's okay." He touched her hand and noticed the slight flinch, the tightening of her lips.

"I talked to Susan. My name is Tom Webb and

I'm—" he laughed at the phrase "—a respected citizen of Cranberry Portage. Susan checked with the Town Clerk and the librarian. They vouched for me. I have a bed-and-breakfast with three empty rooms. The last ones in town. You're all staying with me."

The panic burned brighter, joined by anger. Miranda Jane Roman preferred to be in charge.

"Look. I'll call the nurse. She'll tell you I'm a good guy. If you like I'll get someone to stay in the house with the boys and me. A woman, I mean."

He'd get Mona. Maude would be too busy. Or Lucy, the motherly nurse who worked the front desk in Emergency. He knew her because he'd cut himself half-a-dozen times while working on the house, mostly when Rosa Munde moved his tools, he stumbled over them, or they fell on him from a shelf. Lucy could come over when she got off duty. He'd work something out, even though everyone in town had something to do tonight, some task to perform for the opening ceremonies or tomorrow's party.

Pain overwhelmed the panic in Randy's eyes. He stepped into the hallway and called Lucy, watched while she gave Randy a pill, and then told her about the boys.

Lucy turned back to the bed. "I'll stay at Tom's tonight, but you have to concentrate on getting out of here tomorrow 'cause I'm in the pageant and I can't stay any longer."

The head on the pillow nodded weakly and a faint smile touched her eyes before she closed them. Tom waited to see if they would open again. Five minutes later he heard her breath slow and soften. He touched her cheek, and left to pick up the boys.

Rosa Munde loved the boys. Tom Webb felt the difference as soon as the four of them set foot on the too-long grass at the front of the house. Maybe he could get Eric to cut it while they were here. And that thought led inevitably to one he'd been trying to ignore. How long would they stay?

He knew they were in Cranberry Portage for the re-union. That meant until Tuesday at least. But they had driven all the way from the Coast. Three days seemed like an awful short time to stay for all that work. He reminded himself, not for the first time, that it would be unfair to pump the boys for information while Randy slept in the hospital. He'd told Maude and Mona the same thing. He could only hope, though he doubted it, that they'd listened to him, or, if not, that they wouldn't tell him what they learned.

The problem was twofold. He wanted to know everything there was to know about Miranda Jane Roman so if one of those women phoned him and started talking, he wouldn't be able to resist. But he knew enough about Randy to know how privately she kept herself.

She'd be offended if Tom knew things about her she didn't want him to, or even things she hadn't told him herself. The look in her eyes when he told her he'd phoned Susan alerted him to that. He wouldn't answer the phone tonight; that was the answer.

Rosa Munde looked her best in the hot afternoon sun, her walls and porch dappled with shade from the trees surrounding her. The shade camouflaged the peeling paint. Tom was glad he'd found the time to fix the porch and the swing, time to replace the few rotting floorboards, time to stain and varnish the railings, time to polish Rosa Munde's sign before he left for Winnipeg. She looked pretty good.

And felt good, too. The doors opened without creaking and the rooms felt cool and airy. One of her tricks over the summer had been to start the furnace while he was out so he returned to hot, sticky rooms which took all night to cool. He felt her smile at the energy emanating from the boys.

The three of them—Eric, Mickey, Dexter—had enough energy to send a rocket to the moon. And bring it back.

"Can we see the rest of the house?" Mickey practically bounced on the oak floor. "And the bats?"

He'd told them about the bats on the drive to the hospital, mostly to keep their minds off Randy, who was trying not to moan in the front seat. He talked for the entire hour and a half, about Rosa Munde, the fact she was alive and what that meant while he renovated her. He talked about the bats, about the reunion, about the canoes on the roof of the truck, about his plans for the future.

Randy didn't seem to take in much of it, but the boys did. And they asked questions, hundreds of them, so he just kept talking. Better that than watching her white face, listening to the pain in her breathing, and not being able to do anything about it. That hurt.

Because he wanted to help her. The glass, though, had been in too deep. When she fell, she had pushed the tiny pellets right under the skin. He imagined it felt like buckshot but sharper. As a teenager, he'd caught a few pellets from a poor-sighted hunter. He still remembered what it felt like, those little balls moving around under his skin, the pain when they shifted.

He gave Eric and Mickey a quick guided tour of the house, showed them their basically empty bedrooms, and then set them to unloading the truck while he made arrangements to have Randy's car picked up and repaired.

Gus said, "It'll take a few days to get a windshield up from the city, but I'll start working on the dents right away."

Tom Webb smiled to himself. Gus's few days usually stretched out to a week. He was a prime example of what Tom had labeled Portage Summer Time. Summer was for playing, winter for working. So work, if it threatened to interfere with play, got relegated to second place. Randy's windshield wouldn't get ordered or her car repairs even looked at until after the reunion. That gave Tom a little more time. He'd need it, too.

The unloading of the truck went quickly, even with the addition of everything out of Randy's car. He helped the boys carry it up to the three bedrooms on the third floor. The things that didn't belong to either of them went into what Tom already thought of as Randy's room. Boxes of books, a suitcase, a couple of small bags, a gray plastic tub which looked like nothing he'd ever seen before and felt, when he shook it, like sand or gravel or… He placed it on the windowsill, took a quick glance around the room, then stepped out and closed the door behind him.

Mickey's door was open and the boy sat in the middle of the bed with Dexter beside him, boxes of jam jars piled around them like a miniature fort.

"Look," he said, opening the lid of one of the boxes and holding a jar out to Tom.

The jar contained dragonfly wings. The label said "Highway 1, outside Moosomin," and an unreadable date.

Mickey spread out his arms. "I collected them the whole way. I'm going to collect them on the way home, too. I'll study them when I get home. Maybe there's a pattern."

The boy's eyes shone at the idea, and Tom had to stop himself from reaching over and ruffling his hair, settling instead for a pat on Dexter's head.

"I bet there is a pattern. That's the thing about nature. The pattern is always there, but only certain people can see it. They're the lucky ones. Darwin, Cousteau, Mendel. They saw more than just tortoises or fish or pea plants. They saw the way the world really works and you will, too, if you look for it."

Mickey smiled at Tom as if he'd received a gift.

"Take a break. We'll head downtown around six. I'll be downstairs."

Tom paused at Eric's closed door. He lifted his hand to knock but decided against it. The kid was probably just happy to have some time and space to himself. Tom remembered being sixteen and the stress he felt when too many people were around. He'd leave Eric alone.

The house settled into afternoon slumber and although it was quiet, it was different now. Tom wasn't lonely, or even alone, anymore. The house was full of life. He heard the creak of Eric's footsteps on his way to the bathroom, the faint whoosh of water running, Dexter's soft bark when Eric passed Mickey's room, the rattle of the window sashes, the oiled whir of doors opening and shutting. Tom sat on the porch swing and closed his eyes. The old house was finally a home.

CHAPTER 20

Keep your specimens alive until you arrive home, then quickly relax and mount them. Keeping them alive until you arrive home allows time for the insect to empty its digestive tract, leaving you with a brighter-colored specimen.

—*The Sunshine Coast News*, September 14, 2005

It was quiet in this room, unlike Saint Paul's, where the impersonal sounds of car horns and ambulance sirens fought with crying, the rapid click-click of cheap wheelchairs moving across linoleum, the aged intercom's incessant panicky calls; Saint Paul's, where my mother died and my sister lost her breasts. I looked down at the curve of my breasts beneath the thin blue blanket. I touched them, pushing them together to form a single platform of supposedly disease-free flesh, making sure they were still here, still with me. At least the blanket was the same, though the smell, too, was different, the windows open to dispel the scents of disinfectant and death, letting in the sweet aroma of August.

My nose recognized the combination of baked earth and pollen and fresh-mowed grass despite the passing of the years, and it brought back, like none of the reunion newsletters or my mother's reminiscences had done, the dream of my childhood.

I didn't dare call it memory. I only had two of those and I didn't want to confuse this sensation, because that's all it was, with those precious glimpses of my father. This feeling made me nostalgic for summer. For the baked heat of August when my body held all the warmth of the sun and cold became impossible to imagine. When I moved through the house seeking pockets of light, traveling with the sun, curling up on the floor in a patch of sun like a cat, and moving on when it shifted.

It sounded early. *Day of the Triffids* surfaced again but the few noises were normal ones. Besides, I could see, and my watch and clothes were in the bedside locker. I remembered a nurse folding my T-shirt and tut-tutting over the blood. I didn't have enough energy to even think about getting dressed. Someone would show up soon enough with breakfast or a sponge bath or a bedpan. Hospital routine seldom varied.

I stretched, wary of pain. I knew it was still there, sleeping deep beneath my skin, waiting for something to awaken it. The sense memory of it, excruciating, radiating throughout my body, remained with me, as did the humiliating memory of my moaning and screaming. But the pain itself had been transformed overnight into a dull ache in my head and localized tenderness when I moved my hands and knees. They hurt but I would live. I wasn't sure I could stand up.

And what about that man, whatever his name was, who had picked me up and carried me back to the highway, bundled me, the boys, Dexter and all of our belongings into his truck, and then brought me here? And the boys where? Somewhere safe, I thought. I remembered one of the nurses telling me he was okay. And he talked to Susan to get permission for the boys to stay with him overnight.

He was meant to pick me up this morning, though of course not as early as this. I ran my hands through my sweat-sticky hair and wished for a shower. And a mirror. But the aches kept me in bed. Too embarrassing to be found sprawled on the floor with my back and butt exposed.

The hospital morning rolled on. The breakfast carts rattled in the halls, the sound familiar and comforting. I might have been in any motel from here to the Coast, waiting for the boys to wake up and for us to be on our way, listening to the cleaners chat as they moved from room to room.

The sponge bath, lukewarm, erased the stale smells

of fear and pain and sweat. The bowl of oatmeal, an odd summer choice but one that tasted exactly right, filled my stomach and calmed the slight twinge of nausea. The sight of last night's nurse—Lucy—twigged my memory. Tom Webb. The boys were at his bed-and-breakfast.

"Are the boys okay?"

"Mmm-hmm," she said, her hands soft and sure as she brushed the knots out of my hair. "They went to the opening ceremonies last night, so they were still sleeping when I left."

I laughed. "They'd still be sleeping if they'd gone to bed right after dinner. They're sleepers. I don't think they've seen the morning all summer."

"I doubt Tom Webb is the kind of man to waste daylight hours on sleeping."

I shrugged. If Tom Webb could get Eric and Mickey out of bed before noon he was a better man than I.

"Time for you to get up. I brought you some clean clothes."

The thought of neat, tidy Lucy going through my suitcase—filled with dirty clothes, ratty underwear, the smell of my unwashed skin on the fabrics—made me cringe. But she was good. She didn't let me see any disgust on her face. Maybe it came from being a nurse, that perfect acceptance of people as they were. Was it too late? Was I too old to train as a nurse? I wanted—had to—change careers, and nurses were in demand all over the world. I watched Lucy changing the dressings on my knees and fought the upsurge of nausea. Maybe not too late, but definitely not for me.

Lucy stood me up, swaying on my feet, while she helped me dress.

"Go for a walk." She knelt and pulled on my sandals. "Down to the end of the hall and back. Slowly. It'll hurt a little but that's mostly stiff muscles. Go on." She waved me away. "You'll feel better."

What I felt was fragile, as if the slightest touch would shatter me into a million pieces, just like the windshield.

I shuffled down the hallway gingerly, expecting each step to produce agony. Except it didn't. My body, my legs and back and shoulders, felt the way they always did after I overexercised. Tight. Stiff. Immovable. Sore, but not painful.

The hall, which had stretched out into eternity when I first stepped into it, now appeared possible, even reasonable. I moved slowly, placing each foot carefully onto the padded linoleum. I didn't want to jar anything. I knew there were stitches beneath the dressings because they pulled each time I flexed my knees.

I moved slowly. The thought of having to reach out to the wall for balance with my bandaged hands made me shiver. I couldn't move them without pain, for they had taken the worst of it. So I teetered down the hall like a very old lady or one of those walking dolls I had wished for as a child, each time one of the legs moved the doll tottered, on the verge of falling.

I'd wanted the doll, curly blond hair, royal-blue satin dress festooned with white lace and blue eyes to match her dress, with an ardor verging on unreason. It was the winter after my father had died and we lived in an apartment above a toy store. Alexandria, for I'd named her, sat in the front window of the store and I spent hours with my nose glued to the glass.

What I remembered most about that year wasn't missing my father—it was as if I'd forgotten I ever had one—but that beautiful doll. And the rain. It rained every single day. At least that's what my mother said with a sigh, in the exact same breath as "a little rain won't hurt you," pushing me out the door to school or to hang around in the damp playground, alternately ignored and taunted by my classmates.

Taunted because instead of a bright yellow plastic raincoat and rubber boots, I wore a pea jacket and galoshes, the buckles jingling as I walked. I'd never noticed the sound of those buckles when I lived in Cranberry Portage, but now every step I took was filled with mortification. I begged my mother for rubber boots and for Alexandria. I finally got rubber boots after I grew out of my galoshes, but someone else took Alexandria home. One morning just before Christmas she disappeared from the window and I never saw her again.

Being different—dressing all wrong, using the wrong words for things, wearing galoshes instead of boots, starting school in the middle of the year, and most of all having no father—meant I had no friends. Every morning I walked to school by myself. During recess, I stood with my back to the chain-link fence and watched everyone else running and yelling. Lunch I spent in the library. After school I walked home, galoshes jingling, alone again. But I always had a book or two in my bag. Even when the spring arrived and I put away my galoshes, I still sat in the library, books piled up around me and my head down so no one would notice me.

And that worked all through the first year. I was invisible once I stopped wearing galoshes and what I learned that year stayed with me. Don't stand out, don't be different. And I learned, too, that books would always take me away. Books were my vacations, my solace, my joy, and especially in those early years, my teachers. Because it wasn't until Grade 5 that a teacher—Miss Howick, the only teacher whose name I remembered—realized I couldn't see the blackboard, and called my mother to have my eyes tested.

Suddenly, I saw the kids around me, and the questions on the board. I didn't have to hold my books three inches from my face or lean down and put my face on my desk to write in my scribbler. Being called four-eyes was a small price to pay for the freedom those glasses gave me. Besides, I'd been a solitary kid for all those years. I was used to it. Until I met Patty.

She was the tallest kid in class and I was the shortest. We must have looked like fools walking home together, but from the minute we met we were hardly ever apart. And Patty had plenty of friends so I, her best friend, did too. Once I learned how to have friends, things changed for me. Oh, I still read books, but only when my mother made me stay home to look after Susan. The rest of the time I was out. Rain, shine, didn't matter. And when we moved to another school district, which we did at least once a year, I remembered Patty and made other friends.

But as easy as making friends was, keeping them was impossible. I got used to that as well, and as I grew up, I told myself it was good. I never got bored, never complacent, always moving on.

Moving was my life. New friends, new house or apartment, more or less furniture. Between the time I left home for college and the time Mickey was born I moved at least once a year. In the worst years, I moved two or three times. I was following my mother's pattern—up to the top of the rent scale, then quickly back down to the bottom. I owned nothing that didn't fit in a box or come apart to be carried by one person. But Eric and Mickey changed that. I wanted to be settled for them. I wanted them to have their own rooms when they came to visit. I wanted them to know where I was.

So I stopped moving and started getting anxious. Another revelation? Maybe, but I didn't care. I was getting sick of self-examination. I wanted out of the hospital. I wanted to get back in the car. I wanted to be home, to see Susan, to settle back into my old life. And I wanted to do it now.

I paced the hallway, waiting impatiently for Tom Webb. The sun heated the corridor, warming it like a glass fishbowl, shining directly into the windows by the time he arrived. Without the boys.

"Where are they?" I was pissed off, sore, tired of waiting. He must have heard all of those things in my voice.

"They're in the truck. I wanted to make sure you were okay because they were worried about you. If you weren't okay, I didn't want them to see you."

I tried to keep the anger from my voice. How dare he make decisions about my nephews? "Let's go. I'm fine. I've already signed out."

The trip out to the truck hurt. I'd been pacing for long enough that the muscles had first softened, grown more relaxed, and then restiffened, harder and sorer than ever. Plus the stress on the stitches of my knees made them feel like pincushions poked by dozens of tiny pins and needles. Ouch. But I masked the pain, my cheerful face coming in handy yet again.

The big red truck waited, boy-less, at the curb.

"In the truck, you said?" I stared pointedly at the empty cab.

"They're around here somewhere."

The parking lot and sidewalk were empty. Heat swirls, mirages of water or dust or extra bright light, moved across the asphalt and concrete. But no boys. Or Dexter.

"Did you bring the dog?"

"Yeah." His face brightened. "They've probably taken him for a walk."

I brought my index fingers to my lips and whistled. Dexter raced out from behind the next building over, heading directly for me. I shut my eyes, bracing myself for impact. Nothing.

"Down, boy," I heard. I laughed, closed my eyes tighter, braced myself again. When I opened my eyes, I found Dexter sprawled at Tom Webb's feet, tongue hanging out, and a pair of doggy eyes fixed with adoration on the man's face. That was the final straw.

"Get me the hell out of here. I need to get my car fixed. And I need to find a motel. Now."

I scrambled ignominiously into the cab of the truck and tried to sit regally austere, waiting for the rest of them to join me. I was going to get away from Tom Webb and I was going to do it as soon as possible.

CHAPTER 21

Immediately make notes of where and when you find your specimens. Memory is an unreliable way to collect data.
—*The Sunshine Coast News*, September 14, 2005

Leaving Tom Webb wasn't quite as simple as I'd expected. In fact, the way he, the boys and everyone else in town explained it, the thing was impossible. The boys were settled, unpacked, and busy exploring Cranberry Portage and making plans. With that man. Maude, Town Clerk and chief booking agent, assured me, while winking over my shoulder, that there wasn't another place to stay in the whole town. Because of the reunion, of course. And every other person I ran into told me it was the best thing that could have happened. Fate. Kismet. My good luck. That's what Susan said when I phoned her.

"Does he look as good as he sounds? Stay longer, sweetie, if you want. If you stay another week or ten days, I'll be almost back to normal by the time you get back."

Good luck. Fate. Kismet. Huh. Tom Webb stole my nephews, but I knew I'd get them back once we went home. What really irked me was he stole my house. And he named her Rosa Munde. Damn. Damn. Damn.

Could you call the whole thing a coincidence? Starting with Susan's cancer, losing my job, the trip, the hailstorm, Tom Webb appearing at exactly the right moment? Having quit his job because he'd seen the house once, in the dark of night, for a few short moments? Oh, yes, I knew his story, too. I heard it from Maude, from the boys, from the woman who owned the Coffee Shop. Everyone, that is, except Tom Webb. Because I refused to let him talk to me. And I didn't talk to him.

I didn't believe in fate or coincidence. I made my own luck. Always had. So mostly I tried not to think about what had happened. Although, like leaving Tom Webb and Rosa Munde, it wasn't easy. The whole town knew the story and they thought it romantic. Maude, as tough as a prairie winter on the outside, harbored a soft heart. She convinced Eric and Mickey, who convinced Susan, that Tom and I were meant for each other. Maybe he believed it, I couldn't tell.

But it didn't work for me. Tom Webb made me mad. When he helped me out of the truck, I shook off his hand, hissing.

"Don't touch me, I can do it myself," as I tripped out

of the truck and barely saved myself, at the cost of my right elbow, from landing on my aching knees.

It pissed me off that he not only knew what to do about my skinned elbow but also that he had the perfect first-aid kit. Everything in its place, nothing expired, all things bright and new in their packaging. Not to mention that he could cook and the boys were happy to eat salads and vegetables and do the dishes afterward.

He had some kind of hold over those boys, some connection I'd lost on this trip and that really angered me. I phoned Susan to whine. She laughed.

"Of course they like him. He's a man. And he lives three thousand miles away. He'll never interfere in their real lives so they're free to listen to him now."

That simpleminded explanation didn't satisfy me.

"So you expect they won't react the same way to Steve?"

"Nope. They'll challenge him, fight him, dislike him, because they'll be jealous and he'll always be around. They do it with me all the time."

"They do?"

"Sure."

"You think Tom's okay?" I didn't know why I asked her that question, no matter what she said I wasn't going to believe her.

"I think he's better than okay. I like him. The boys want him to come out here for Thanksgiving. I asked him."

"What did he say?"

"He said it depends."

"On what?"

"He didn't tell me."

But I could tell from her tone of voice that she had a guess, and, like the women in Cranberry Portage, she thought it had to do with me. And maybe it did, from Tom's point of view, but not from mine.

"If he's there, I won't be. He makes me crazy. I don't like the way he bought the house out from under my nose," ignoring the fact that he did so before I'd even remembered it existed. "I don't like the way he's fixed it up," even though he'd done everything I would have, "and I really don't like the way the boys follow him around."

"Oh, Randy…"

"And he's training Dexter."

Susan laughed. I'd spent hours since we found Dexter complaining about his bad behavior and now I complained because someone else had taught him to heel and sit and stay. No wonder she laughed.

"He can't do anything right, can he?"

"He's a good cook."

"That's something."

"Not much. And now he wants to take us on a canoe trip once the reunion is over. He's some high mucky-muck canoe guru and the boys are as keen as…well, you know how they get."

"Perfect. You can get him to take you to Paint Lake."

I didn't answer.

"Randy? I know you're still there, I can hear you breathing. Randy? You are going to take Mum to Paint Lake, aren't you? You promised."

I began the trip with a promise I had no intention of keeping. There remained too many things unresolved between my mother and me for me to scatter her to the prairie winds. Then I'd never get a chance to talk to her. Some of that feeling had changed with the conversations we'd had in the Laundromats but still...I wasn't ready to give her up. Maybe I'd never be.

I left Susan with a sound that might have meant anything. Yes. No. Of course. Maybe. What it meant was I'd see. I'd take her with us on the damn canoe trip and I'd see. What I hoped was it would all come together for me at Paint Lake.

I planned to come to terms with death. My goal for the next week. Simple, huh? My father, my mother, me, Susan, Auntie Mabel. Deaths past and deaths yet to come. So when the boys and Tom went to the reunion—the pancake breakfasts, the pageant, the rodeo, the midway, the country fair, the parade, the nightly fireworks—I stayed home, in the room I pretended had been mine as a child. It might have been. I stayed in my room, my mother in her gray plastic tub on the windowsill, and I concentrated. I tried to use the house as a talisman, rubbing the walls, taking deep breaths, hoping to smell out the past. I even tried what little I knew of yoga.

I wasted hours that way, turning paler as I avoided the sunlight like a vampire. The four walls of my room contained my whole life. The two precious memories of my father, the nights with my mother trembling on the dryer, on the stage with the Sweet Adelines, Auntie Mabel and her stories, Susan on the day I showed up at her graduation, Eric and Mickey in their cribs, in their beds at my house. The summer of Roy, *The Day of the Triffids*, my engagement ring lying on the french-polished table.

I gathered it all around me, all the moments I remembered, all the ones I didn't but made up stories for. I gathered in the journey Eric and Mickey and I had taken—the mornings in the grubby, hot rooms watching them sleep, the long hours on the road, Mickey's face concentrating, his tongue between his teeth, while he pulled wings from the windshield. The dragonflies—on the rock, above the dinosaur museum, in the jars. Dexter. Eric and his silence, encapsulated with the sound of music. I gathered it all together, spinning a tapestry of my life. And at the center, a void.

Because what belonged there was me and I was a blank. I had no idea who I was anymore. No longer a loyal employee of the bank, an upstanding citizen with a house, a car, a mortgage, I was unemployed. No longer the perfect aunt, for hadn't I lost Mickey, and run away, leaving them to fend for themselves in the heart of the prairies? Never a good daughter. Certainly not a wife or a lover. Who was I? Who was I going to be?

The pieces of my life spun around me, faster and faster, while I sat, dizzy and nauseous in the middle, trying desperately to find a place for myself, a meaning.

Tom or one of the boys brought my meals to me on a tray, told me where they'd been, where they were going. I ate, absentmindedly, watching the movie of my life. I fast-forwarded through the truly painful scenes, paused sometimes to examine more carefully a moment I'd forgotten, rewinding to go over and over something I didn't understand. None of it helped.

Mickey, Eric and Dexter, meanwhile, were having the time of their lives. They were stars to the residents of Cranberry Portage. They had stories to tell, about Susan, about their grandmother, about their trip across the continent. About me.

And I knew those stories, had their voices stuck in my head, spent hours imagining how badly I appeared to the people who lived in my childhood home. The aunt who just missed killing all of us on the Saskatchewan highway, who vanished in the night, leaving them to the mercy of oil-pigs, who lost Mickey in an unknown town in the heart of the Rockies.

A woman entering middle age without a job or a man or a future. Oh, yes, they definitely had stories to tell. They were sympathetic creatures, my nephews, and so they should be, I thought. For all the stories they had to tell were true. All the stories they told formed part of the movie of my life.

It was as if their stories about me were true, real in a way that my memories, both real and manufactured, were not. Somehow, in the act of telling, Eric and Mickey solidified the facts, brought them into a form of reality I was incapable of accomplishing on my own. Reality. What difference did that make? If I remembered something, that was all that counted. Right?

It used to be right until this journey. I used to believe, after half-a-dozen retellings, in the stories I created to replace the memories I didn't have. But now I knew the difference. Those two small memories of my father felt true in a way my stories didn't, felt true and real in the same way the stories told by Eric and Mickey did in comparison to me telling the same stories. I'd lost half of my life and had only one bowl of popcorn and one cool autumn morning to replace it.

After two days in my room trying to resolve this dilemma, I gave up. My mother wasn't talking, my life wasn't getting any better, and I was getting tired of picking the scabs off my knees. I still didn't know if I'd be able to scatter my mother's ashes on Paint Lake and the thought of Tom Webb still made me mad. But I abandoned my stint as the Lady in the Tower and headed off into Cranberry Portage.

I caught up with the four of them in the sawdust around the rodeo ring. The residents of Cranberry Portage had taken advantage of the already-contracted- for rodeo ring and booked in a week of bull riding after the reunion. In fact, even though I'd missed the official reunion, the unofficial one looked to be going on for the whole summer. They stood, the three humans with one foot each on the bottom rail of the fence, Dexter on a very short lead held very tightly by Eric, all of them engrossed by a huge angry bull separated from them by a weak fence.

"Wow," Mickey said, "look at his eyes. He's mad."

"His skin doesn't fit him. It's like he's lost a thousand pounds, no wonder he's mad. Do you think…" Eric started to scramble through the fence, but got no farther than a single arm before Tom yanked him back.

"I don't care what it feels like. If you want to touch his skin we'll wait until he's in the chute and see if the handlers will let you in then."

I'd come upon the scene prepared to do battle, another mistake made by Tom Webb, endangering Eric's life, yet he'd dealt with it better than I could have. The man was a damn saint. That made me even angrier.

The weight of my fury must have burned a hole through his back. He turned and saw me, nudged the boys. All three of them started toward me across the sawdust, their faces lit with identical grins. What in the hell was I going to do?

Go with the flow, it appeared, as I followed them across the landscape of Cranberry Portage in the summer, putting in twelve-hour days at breakfasts, canoe challenges, amateur bronc-riding (which all three of them loved and I couldn't watch, hiding my face in my hands waiting for the solid splotch signaling broken bones and another quick trip to the hospital), feasts and line dancing. Every nationality (and there were dozens) represented in Cranberry Portage had booths full of food. We ate cabbage rolls, tortiere, souvlaki, chop suey, beaver tails (not the real ones, the cinnamon-and-sugar kind), pasta, bannock, and several things for which I didn't know the names or ingredients. And the boys ate it all. They didn't show a hint of the fussiness that had us eating fast food right across the country.

A week later I was exhausted. I'd been spared the endless round of handshakes but not the reminiscences. I heard stories of my childhood, of my mother's childhood, even a few stories about my grandmother's childhood. I heard stories about Susan, about the two of us together, and most of all I heard stories about my father. Mum and Susan and I were minor characters compared to his place in the saga of Cranberry Portage.

Like Elvis and JFK and Marilyn Monroe, his mysterious death at such a young age put him in the pantheon of superstars. Everything he'd ever done, every car he drove, every jacket or tire or pair of boxer shorts he bought, every sniffle or cough, were all remembered and regurgitated to me. They told me about the year he learned to curl, and how he could skate and shoot like Davey Keon. They told me the size of his feet and that he was bow-legged, and though they'd speculated, they told me they didn't know why he died or how.

I brought the stories back with me to Rosa Munde and late at night, the boys and Dexter and Tom Webb asleep in the rooms around me, I repeated them to my mother. I told her every single thing they told me. I talked until my throat hurt and my eyes felt full of sand.

And then I lay down under the comforter chosen by Tom Webb and replayed the stories again, this time in real time, with a speaking, walking, live little girl playing the role of Miranda Jane Roman. Daughter of the man who died, tragically, one cool sunny autumn day, a day no one in Cranberry Portage would ever forget. And as I repeated the stories, first to my mother and then to myself, I gradually immersed myself into them.

They grew up around me like beanstalks, taller and more sturdy with each telling. Those stories became a part of me, of my past, of my life. I didn't just retell them, I relived them. Maybe they were false memories, maybe they weren't really mine, but I made them so.

For the first time I knew my father and I knew myself, that small child holding her father's hand while he laughed with the clerk at the hardware store. The little girl who learned to ride her first bike with the help of half the town—was *me*. I told myself into that story. The girl who lost the spelling bee because she couldn't spell *because*. Those girls were me.

Telling the stories made me feel at home. Telling the stories to my mother made me feel like an adult. Suddenly I knew I could keep my promise to Susan. I would talk to Tom Webb about it in the morning. I watched as the sun sailed across the sky and fell off the edge of the earth, leaving only darkness, into which I traveled to sleep.

Eric's Notebook

Paint Lake. I looked it up on Tom's map. It's a long trip. Two or three days each way. A couple of portages. We'll have to take two canoes and Randy won't be any help. Her hands still hurt. I can see by the way she moves. I hope she goes in Tom's canoe. That way I don't have to watch over her all the time. I'm tired of it.

I know why we're going. She thinks it's a secret. But some nights when she left the motel room I followed her. Watched through the windows. She talked to Mum on the phone. And then she talked to the gray tub. And that's Grandma. I know because Mum told me.

Mum told me to look after Mickey. And she told me we had to go even though I wanted to stay and look after her. She wanted Grandma's ashes out of Randy's house. She thought it was weird to keep them for so long.

If she thought that was weird, she should see things now. Maybe not right now. Randy's been okay for the last couple of days. But before that? Mega-weird. She talked all day and all night to those ashes. I couldn't hear what she said. I'm glad I couldn't. It's kind of scary. I'm glad Tom's here. And I'm glad we're going to get rid of them before we go home. Really glad.

I don't want them in the car with me again. They've gotta go before we go home.

CHAPTER 22

...the waters are hungry, and the bottom are a naked sand.
—Gilbert H. White

Paint Lake. Tom Webb had always wanted to see it and now he was on his way. And for the first time he traveled with companions—four of them.

Eric, Mickey and Dexter were excited, exuberant in the way only adolescents achieved. Tom remembered feeling the same way, as if he moved in air filled with bubbles, champagne or ginger ale—his body tingled, warmed, caressed with each step until he didn't know whether to laugh or run. Only that he needed to do something, anything, to acknowledge the sensation. Something physical, preferably, fast and loud and annoying to everyone around him. It was an incredible feeling, but short-lived. He delighted in the three of them and enjoyed watching them try to release that energy. The trip would be good for them.

Randy was the question mark. She seemed okay on the way home from the hospital, making sure the boys were in good hands, checking out the house and Tom. He'd never been so carefully scrutinized and questioned. Not by prospective employers or women or even bank managers. Miranda Jane Roman was good. And tough. But she disappeared in on herself after he brought her home to Rosa Munde.

When she finally left her room after three days inside, she had changed in some indefinable way. That fire, anger mostly, he'd thought, had been banked down, like a campfire at night. So Tom had no idea what would happen over the next five days. He would spend it in the August sun, on the water, with an interesting woman, two teenagers, and an adolescent dog. Something was sure to explode. He smiled at the thought of it.

The old red truck waited in the driveway, festooned with canoes and life jackets, paddles and kit bags. Coolers—one for each canoe—sat on the kitchen table together with a sturdy black backpack. Tom stood next to them with a checklist, overseeing the packing.

"Why are we taking these?" Mickey asked, holding up a Ziploc bag full of cotton balls.

"Those go in the black bag."

"Yeah, okay, but why?"

"They're good kindling."

"Oh. Okay. These too?"

"Yep."

A small bag of finely shredded twigs went into the backpack, and another Ziploc bag with candles and matches. Tom watched while Mickey picked up a squirt bottle and sniffed it.

"That's awful."

"Ammonia," Tom said. "A drop in a Ziploc bag and then in with the food. Bear-proofing."

Eric rummaged in the fridge, Dexter drooling at his heels. Tom's instructions had been clear. Fruit, vegetables, mustard, ketchup. But Eric's arms, and the kitchen table, contained all sorts of other things. Orange and apple juice, bottles of pop and jars of pickles.

"Nothing goes in that isn't plastic."

"No pickles?"

"Not unless you put them in Ziploc bags."

Eric looked at the jar and the boxes of bags on the counter. Tom felt him considering the amount of work involved. Was it worth it to him? Nope. The pickles went back in the fridge with the bottles of pop.

"Why not the pop? They're in plastic bottles."

"Too heavy. I'll drink water instead."

Tom and Eric had spent the evening before at the kitchen table with maps and guidebooks spread out in front of them. They worked out a route, calculated the portages, argued good-humoredly about how much food and water they needed—making one quick run to the store for more chocolate for inspiration—and continued arguing about how long each leg of the trip would take. In each case, Tom went conservative, Eric in the opposite direction.

"We can do this in three hours," Eric said, pointing at a long, straight segment.

"Yeah, if we paddle like we're in a dragon-boat race and have been training flat out for six months. Six hours, easy."

They compromised on everything, Tom listening to Eric and giving in when he could—in that instance they calculated five hours—and Tom silently added the one hour to the other hours he'd allowed Eric. Three unknown paddlers with Randy's hands still in bandages.

He made sure his list, and the final packing, took account of everything that might go wrong. Because at least half of what he could imagine was sure to go wrong. It was going to be great experience for next summer when he started his official career as a guide. He'd get it right or die trying.

In the days before they left, he often thought of Randy's father. He'd been an experienced paddler, an avid and careful outdoorsman, but something had happened. He had made the wrong decision. Maybe he forgot to plan for it, or maybe he simply got careless. Maybe Paint Lake felt so familiar, so safe, he forgot to be careful. And the wilderness got him, as it got lots of people who lost their sense of caution.

Tom knew how easy it was to believe you were safe. He'd heard dozens of people say, "We're just going for a couple of hours," and shrug when he mentioned survival gear. And he'd been on plenty of search parties looking for those same people two days later when they got lost or injured or dead.

He'd been there himself, once. Twenty years ago. Remembering that trip became part of his planning, a sort of subliminal warning: *This is where arrogance gets you.* A litany of all the things that could, and mostly did, go wrong. Weather was the first thing. He hadn't checked the forecast and was quickly enveloped in a late spring blizzard. He hadn't packed a compass. Or a change of clothes or a candle or matches or a magnifying glass. No space blanket, no kindling. Just Tom Webb, his canoe, a six-pack of beer and a couple of tuna-fish sandwiches.

He'd been lucky, found a sheltered bay and stayed there until they found him, but you couldn't count on that. His frostbitten toes and fingertips reminded him of that every year when the temperature dropped. No, Tom Webb no longer believed in luck. Now he believed in planning. And plenty of garlic sausage and cheese and thick black Winnipeg rye bread. He believed in a well-thought-out and packed survival bag. He believed in maps and compasses and a GPS. He believed in safety and in patience. Don't rush, don't panic. Tom Webb's philosophy of life.

Eric pulled another bag from the fridge. A look of disgust settled over his face. His nose wrinkled as he quickly set the bag back in the fridge and slammed the door behind it.

"Garlic sausage," Tom said. "No matter how you wrap it, it still smells. We'll put it in another couple of bags before it goes in the cooler."

"We're taking that with us?"

"Yep. It's the best camping food there is. Except for M&M's."

Eric smiled at that. He's a good kid, Tom thought. So was Mickey. They'd be fine traveling companions.

"I'm going to phone Mum before we go. Come on, Mickey."

That left Tom alone in the kitchen. He raced through the rest of the packing, doubling up on everything on the list, just as he'd done last night with the things already in the truck. He had waited until Eric was asleep. He wouldn't hurt the boy's feelings, but he wouldn't travel without enough supplies, either.

When he looked up from the cooler, Randy was slouched in the doorway, her hair still damp from the shower. The bandages on her knees and hands were smaller this morning.

"I changed them after I got out of the shower. They don't hurt much anymore."

Tom shrugged, embarrassed she'd read his mind so easily and worried about what else she saw when she looked at him.

"Coffee?"

"Thanks. What are we doing about breakfast? Should I make something? Pancakes? Eggs?"

"No. We'll go out so we don't have to worry about dishes. I'll just take these to the truck and we're ready."

Tom grabbed one of the coolers and the black bag, Randy following with the other cooler. She grunted with pain as she picked it up but kept on. He didn't turn around, just hoped she wasn't doing any serious damage to herself. When she passed the cooler up to him in the truck, he surreptitiously checked the bandages. Not surreptitiously enough.

"No blood," she said, holding up her hands. "The wounds are pretty much healed. I just put bandages on 'cause they're still kind of tender."

"Good." He couldn't think of anything else to say.

"I won't be a hindrance," she said fiercely. "I won't. I'll paddle, too."

Tom kept the grin from his face with difficulty. He hadn't expected anything less. She was tough and damned independent. He'd have to watch she didn't overdo it trying to keep up. Because she would, he knew that about her. She didn't want to owe anybody anything, especially not, for some reason, him. They'd already fought about the trip.

She wanted to pay for it: he wouldn't let her. He made a mental note to check the house and truck for envelopes before they left rather than after. He wouldn't put it past her to leave cash—he wondered how she valued his services and was tempted for a minute to open the envelope when he found it—somewhere out of the way, hoping he wouldn't find it until they were gone back to the Coast.

But she didn't know Tom Webb very well, not yet. He'd already got her address from Susan and would have no hesitation about sending her money back. Or delivering it himself.

"I'll go wake up the boys," she said, pulling him out of a daydream of standing on her front porch with a white envelope in his hand. Unopened.

Tom Webb watched Randy's face as he told her the boys were already up. The anger was clear, creasing across her forehead. She was pissed off because they woke up early and willingly for him. The same hadn't been true while she traveled with them. The sadness wasn't quite so obvious but it was there, in the slight downturn of her mouth, in the lowering of her eyelids. She felt she'd lost the boys to Tom. He knew that wasn't true, though he didn't know how to tell her so. They'd grown up in a world of women—Susan, Randy, their grandmother—Tom was a novelty to them. They liked him, enjoyed his company, but they loved Randy.

"I don't know how you do it," she said. "I've been dragging them out of bed at noon most days."

Tom respected her for that comment, acknowledging something so painful. He pondered his answer. The last thing he wanted to do…what was the last thing he wanted to do? Oh, yeah. The last thing he wanted to do was to hurt Randy. And the first thing he wanted to do was kiss her. He compromised, reaching out a hand to help her down from the truck bed.

"It's not me, you know. It's the trip."

"What about the past week? We've been in Cranberry Portage for a week, no trip then. No, it's you. Something about you."

"Yeah, I'm a man." He spit it out without thinking and immediately regretted it.

She chewed on that for a while, her head bowed. It was as if she suddenly realized a truth so huge it overwhelmed her. When she finally raised her head, her eyes were full of tears. She ignored them.

"Thanks." She looked at the packed truck, then back at him. "Call them, will you? Let's get going."

He didn't need to call the boys. He'd seen them out of the corner of his eye while he talked to Randy, had warned them to stay away with a flick of his hand. But he whistled just the same. They galloped up, loud, boisterous, excited. Randy touched her fingers to her eyes and smiled at them.

"I'm going back up to lock the doors, check the stove. Five minutes." He glared at Mickey. "Don't go anywhere. And put that leash on Dexter. When I get back we're off and whoever's not here can go stay with Maude until the rest of us get home."

Everything looked okay at the house. He locked the doors behind him and hurried back down to the truck. It was time to go. He stopped at the foot of the yard. Randy, Eric and Mickey sat on the curb next to the truck, deep in conversation. Tom sat on the steps down to the road and waited. He heard Randy's voice.

"I know this has been a rough trip, for me too. Maybe me especially. And I'm sorry. I should have done things differently."

The boys said nothing, their stillness almost uncanny, waiting, the only motion their hair moving slightly in the breeze. Randy cleared her throat, squared her shoulders.

"Your mum isn't going to die. I don't know why I couldn't tell you that before, couldn't reassure you. I guess I was too scared. About losing my job, about your mum, about being alone with the two of you. About almost everything, I guess. But she's not going to die. I talked to her, and I talked to Steve, and I phoned the cancer clinic this morning just to be sure. Everyone told me that all the tests are clear."

She waited, again, for them to say something. Still no words but a tiny movement of Mickey's shoulders, curling and relaxing.

"I'm sorry I've been such a mess this summer, but everything's going to be okay. For all of us."

She said that with such confidence, Tom thought. She really believed it. Which was kind of funny since he was positive she hadn't believed any such thing even this morning.

"Mum's going to meet us here. She and Steve are driving out," Mickey said. "She told me this morning."

Tom stood up and strode over to where the three of them sat. They looked up at him, hands shielding their eyes from the sun.

"So we'd better get going, huh? Or we won't be back in time."

CHAPTER 23

Dragonflies have been seen by many cultures as
omens, their flashing wings and bright colors a sign
of hope, but to entomologists, they are just bugs.
—*The Sunshine Coast News*, September 14, 2005

P aint Lake. It's as if I've been heading there all my life,
as if everything I've done has been calculated to lead
me to this place, to my past. I know I'll be disappointed.
Because it cannot be as beautiful as my mother has
said, as my father might have said to me in dreams, as
I have imagined it. But now I'm sitting on a log by the
lake and it's as beautiful as I could have imagined. More
beautiful than anywhere.

It shines a cool turquoise in the late-afternoon sun.
A raft of cinnamon teals huddle in a tight scrum near
the shore, shifting slightly when I move. The silence,
solid and thick with the summer heat, enfolds me and
through it I hear only small sounds: the ruffling of feath-
ers; a drop of water from an unfolding wing hitting the

still surface of the lake; the distant caw of a crow; the susurration of my own breath.

The water is clear. I see the mottled gray rocks on the lake bed as it slopes away from the shore. I want to step into the water and pick them up in my hands, caress their smoothness, the cool sensual shapes of them.

Tom and the boys are setting up camp behind me. They unloaded the canoes, leaving them on the beach near where I sit. One thing remains in the red canoe, a gray plastic tub casting a shadow across the thwart.

I hear Tom's footsteps long before he reaches me. I have time to ready myself, although I know it won't help. I don't know how to answer the question he is going to ask me. He sits on the log a carefully calculated distance away. Not too close; he knows I'll move. Not too far; he wants to be able to touch me.

"Do you want us to come with you?" His suntanned face is hopeful beneath the hat brim.

"I don't know."

"The boys would like to be there. Susan would like them to be there."

My nod in response is only an acknowledgment of their wanting, not a consent to it. Because this is my job to do and having them with me might dilute the satisfaction I'll get doing it. What I do want is not to make a decision about this, not today. I'm not ready.

"I don't know," I repeat, to the man waiting patiently by my side.

"Why don't you take a walk before dinner? Think about it. We're going to stay here tonight and most of the day tomorrow."

In order to get back to Cranberry Portage in time to meet Susan and Steve we've had to collapse the trip, starting a little closer to Paint Lake, traveling more quickly, stopping only for the night and not doing any sight-seeing. If this were for any other reason, the boys would be disappointed. Because it's for their mother, I can feel their impatience for the trip to be over. They would prefer to be waiting in Cranberry Portage. A canoe trip at this stage seems frivolous and uncalled-for. They want to be waiting, pacing the front porch, checking their watches, charting the sun as it moves across the sky.

And so their behavior is perfect. They want to get back on time, without accident or delay. And they have switched roles again, which I find disconcerting. Eric is once again the leader, the talker. He sits in the green canoe with all the authority of a park ranger, quietly giving orders to Mickey and Dexter.

"Sit still," he says, and Dexter stops his excited bouncing and sits in the middle of the canoe, only his head and tail visible above its sides.

"Don't splash." Mickey's paddling settles to a steady, almost formal rhythm.

Their green canoe has mostly been in front of our red one, cleaving the way into the wilderness, moving ahead like a lodestar. We follow, careful, without discussion, not to get too close. We have chosen to allow Eric and Mickey the point position, to give them the honor of discovery. They are first.

And much of the time it feels that way. As if we are, have always been, alone in this place of low hills and stunted trees and endless water. It is as empty and silent as it must have been a hundred years before, as it would have been on that September afternoon when my father settled into this lake, falling to sleep on its bosom.

I spend much of my time on this trip to Paint Lake thinking about my father, reliving the few memories I have managed to unearth. Tom is the perfect traveling companion, bending himself to my mood so that we glide through the days in silence, not sullen or sad, but thoughtful. Full of thought, of memory of the past.

Although this journey began as a gift to my sister, the gift of peace for her recovery, it has turned into much more for me. It has been an exploration of my past and with it, my future. I still don't know what I'll do, but I'm no longer worried about it. Somehow the unfettered weeks on the road have released something in me. A willingness, I think, to relax into myself, my life.

So I think about my father and occasionally my mother. And I drift through this northern landscape listening to the lap of the cool water against the canoe, to Tom's murmured instructions, to the faint sounds of laughter from the boys' canoe, almost out of earshot around the next bend.

I think about the task I've come to perform here at journey's end, and I wonder how to do it. And then I lay that thought aside. This trip has taught me that tiny miracles happen almost every day. Until now, I've been too busy to notice. But the unplanned days and the boys have taught me to see them—the dragonfly on the rock; Dexter's appearance in our life; my resurrected memories; Susan's recovery; the hailstorm; being rescued by Tom, a man who lives in my house. I hardly have to enumerate them. They fill my head, rolling over each other like a litter of puppies in a basket, each distinct yet connected, to me and to the others.

Tom is linked to my past—he and Rosa Munde. But is he part of my future? Maybe. He wants to be, I know that. I'll wait and see. See what Susan thinks when she meets him. See what happens when he comes to Vancouver for Thanksgiving.

He is still patiently waiting for me to decide what to do about my mother's ashes. He hasn't started to fidget, just sits looking out at the lake, and I realize, without knowing it, I have decided.

"I'll go on my own. After supper. I'll take the canoe, okay?"

"Of course."

He stands and holds his hand out to help me up from the log. I grasp it and don't want to let go; his strength and warmth are comforting.

The sun is on its downward slide as I walk back down to the beach. I pull the canoe into the water. It is cold, even this late in the summer, and clear.

I begin to stroke, slowly, first one side, then the other. The camp is at my back as I glide through the still water. There are no other people at Paint Lake, no evidence of human occupation, save my canoe and the camp I've left behind. I pass bushes bright with berries beckoning red in the sun. A few poplars stand guard over the edge of the lake, and maples shed the first leaves of the coming fall as I watch.

The circuit of Paint Lake takes me almost two hours. I stop only once—a rocky spit on the far side of the lake across from the camp—the farthest point in my journey. I remove the lid from the gray plastic tub and take my mother in my hands, scoop after scoop. I return her to the arms of my father. I don't speak, not out loud. Everything I needed to say to her has been said, everything I wanted to hear, I have heard.

The camp is almost invisible from this distance, but a faint reflection of light from the fire serves to guide me home.

The pale lemon sun illuminates the tips of the pine

branches, setting the scrub brush aglow as it settles below the horizon. I time my return to that moment when the east side of the lake sinks into darkness, the west side retaining the light, a beacon by which I steer for home.

I move slowly now, my body tired from the long, slow trip around the lake. I pull the canoe from the water to rest on the shore and walk back up the path to the camp.

Tom and Eric and Mickey and Dexter wait for me by the fire. The flames warm their faces. Eric hands me a cup of hot chocolate; Mickey passes me a cushion for my back. Dexter settles at my feet with a sigh while Tom rests his warm hands on my shoulders. I close my eyes and smile.

I am at journey's end.